Pra

"A deeply g...
RICHARD BAUSCH, WINNER, PEN/MALAMUD & REA AWARDS

"Elizabeth Bruce's stories have that rare quality of feeling
as though they have always existed, the way the best
stories always do. These are exquisite short stories that
give me hope."
JOHN MCNALLY, AUTHOR OF *THE BOOK OF RALPH: A NOVEL*

"Inventiveness, voice, and vivid characters grappling with
life and love pour forth on each page. A remarkable tapestry
around a shockingly familiar starting point, this collection
brings us new ways of seeing ourselves and the constella-
tions of our closest relationships. It's breathtaking."
DAVID A. TAYLOR, AUTHOR OF *SOUL OF A PEOPLE: THE WPA
WRITERS' PROJECT UNCOVERS DEPRESSION AMERICA*

"A gifted storyteller, Elizabeth Bruce is at her best here.
Keen-eyed and with a great gift for stand-out narratives at
whose heart is a profound appreciation of the particular,
she takes us on a journey with ordinary people whose lives
turn on a dollar. These stories sing with ingenuity. Just
how far can one dollar take a person? You'd be amazed."
NAOMI AYALA, AUTHOR OF
CALLING HOME: PRAISE SONGS & INCANTATIONS

"Elizabeth Bruce's stories shine a light on the conflicts—big
and small—that we face in life and our struggles to resolve
them. She writes thoughtfully and elegantly about the pain
and beauty of being alive."
ERIC STOVER, FACULTY DIRECTOR, UC HUMAN RIGHTS CENTER,
CO-PRODUCER, PBS DOCUMENTARY,
TULSA: THE FIRE AND THE FORGOTTEN

"In Elizabeth Bruce's hands we learn that the answer to grief is kindness. Instead of pandemic, Bruce offers us a contagion of hope in her wonderful, incredibly humane stories."
NICK KOCZ, WINNER, WASHINGTON SQUARE FICTION AWARD, AUTHOR (AS S.M. THAYER), *I WILL NEVER LEAVE YOU*

"A beautifully crafted gem glittering with wit and insight."
SARAH PLEYDELL, AUTHOR OF *COLOGNE*

"Elizabeth Bruce is the ninja of flash fiction. Her literary precision pierces that tender spot that both stings and satisfies the reader's soul."
JOY JONES, AUTHOR OF *JAYLA JUMPS IN*

"Quintessential Elizabeth Bruce—that rhythm, that wit, that clarity—a song in story form."
KATHLEEN WHEATON, FORMER PRESIDENT, WASHINGTON WRITERS' PUBLISHING HOUSE

"Elizabeth Bruce has the gift of saying more with fewer words, leaving readers everything they need to know while trusting them to assemble the character between the lines."
DANA KING, AUTHOR OF *PENNS RIVER SERIES*

About the Author

Elizabeth Bruce's debut novel, *And Silent Left the Place*, won Washington Writers' Publishing House's Fiction Prize, with *ForeWord Magazine* and Texas Institute of Letters' distinctions. She's published in journals and anthologies around the world. A co-founder of DC's Sanctuary Theatre, she has a long history as a teaching artist, arts producer, and author of CentroNía's *Theatrical Journey Playbook: Introducing Science to Early Learners through Guided Pretend Play*, and currently produces *Creativists in Dialogue: A Podcast Embracing the Creative Life*. A DC-based "Tex-pat," she's received DC Commission on the Arts & Humanities, HumanitiesDC, and McCarthey Dressman Education Foundation fellowships and studied with Richard Bausch, the late Lee K. Abbott, Janet Peery, John McNally, and Liam Callanan.

elizabethbrucedc.com

UNI VERS ALLY ADORED

and Other $1 Dollar Stories

Elizabeth Bruce

www.vineleavespress.com

Author photograph by Nicolas Ortega-Ward.

Cover design by Jessica Bell
Interior design by Amie McCracken

To Gladys

Contents

Couples

Sweat

One dollar.

The old woman pressed the worn bill between her hands. She raised it to her cheek beneath the eyes that no longer saw. Rumpled, an old bill.

Old like we became.

She found its corners, one dog-eared, another torn, and touched them to her lips. A benediction.

It smelled faintly of sweat.

Whose sweat, is it mine? Lord, I have shed some sweat in my time.

Or his, bending his back against the torments of the sun, sweat darkening the small of his back, under his arms, across his neck?

Man sweat, rough and sweet.

Sweet, like the whispers they had made together, even there near the end before he passed, before his body, spent and curled, faded, before he had called her to him and given her the dollar.

"My last dollar, sweetheart." He had gathered his last words like the posies he used to pick for her. "First, last, and every dollar in between," he'd whispered. "They were all for you, darlin'."

The old woman felt the corners of the bill and folded it over into itself, as his old body had done there at the end, as her old body was doing now without him. She held the bill close as she'd held him one final time and tucked it into the pocket above her heart.

Universally Adored

Dedicated to J.S.G. Boggs and Hans-Jürgen Kuhl
(among other "counterfeiters")

One dollar. American.

Fran stares at the Christmas card from Janine that came that morning, addressed in the loopy, backward-slanted handwriting she'd know anywhere. *A card from Janine? Is it possible?* Santa's sled arches over the Las Vegas strip, money floating down like snowflakes, one huge dollar bill in the foreground.

Swimming in the green stuff, Janine had written on the inside, and in parentheses she'd added: *(prettiest color I ever saw!)* with a silly happy face after it.

Fran runs her thumb over the card's vellum paper. Velvety. Soft. Soft like Janine. She looks at the faint gray lines that ripple across the Forever stamp flag's red, white, and blue. *Las Vegas, Nevada,* says the postmark.

Las Vegas. Sin City. Janine's sister lives there. The day Janine walked out, her sister drove down from Vegas and loaded up her station wagon with the detritus of Janine's two years with Fran.

Silver. The station wagon was silver, like a bullet to the heart.

"Screw it," Janine said that day, with a violence that shook Fran out of the closet art studio where she hovered most days, made her drop the palomino-colored oil pastel secretly named Janine to the eighth power and run trembling to where Janine stood in the living room, next to the picture that Fran had first given her.

A cold dread filtered in that day, slithering over Fran's slippers and up the legs of her jeans.

"Screw you and your goddamn art. I am done here," Janine shouted as she filled the boxes with her wander yearnings from their years together, the phrase books and guides to countries they'd never managed to visit after all. Never could afford it.

The dread wrapped itself around Fran's chest, tightening. *This can't be happening.*

Janine knocked the abstract blue painting she had once adored off the wall, the glass in its frame shattering and scattering slivers of translucence across the wooden floor.

Fran gasped and knelt to rescue it. It had brought them together, this painting, with its cascade of shades, and now it was on the floor. What had she done so wrong?

"Keep it," Janine shouted. "Keep your goddamned blue swirly whirls and all the rest of this crap," she yelled, sweeping her arm over the shelf of mementos Fran had bought for them at garage sales and flea markets, each with its own astonishing color field and texture.

The oxidized copper ladle, the cocktail tray filled with butterfly wings, the intricately woven Peruvian belt, the turquoise porcelain sake cup. Visual treasures, Fran called them, and she thought they were Janine's treasures too, things they could enjoy together.

"Keep all of your damn colors," Janine shouted. And with that she kicked the first box out of the apartment and slammed the old door, flecks of avocado paint flying off like bits of dusty cactus.

One by one Janine dragged the cardboard boxes, their sides buckling, down the four flights of stairs into the station wagon below.

Thump, step, thump, step, thump, step, thump, went the boxes as Janine wrestled them out of her life with Fran. They sounded to Fran like the clunk, clunk, clunks of red clay hitting a casket below.

I should have helped Janine, Fran thinks again, alone now in the apartment. Helped her lug those soft brown boxes down the steps, but Janine was so angry, so very angry, that Fran was afraid to even try. Her beautiful Janine had turned on her, and Fran struggled to understand why.

Janine was months gone now, all her things thumped, thumped to the street, and off to her sister's house in Vegas. Her sister got her a job as a blackjack dealer, last Fran heard, and she's finally making good money. Not like Fran, limping along on her meager sidewalk art sales and money from her mom to keep the landlord at bay.

Fran closes her eyes and thinks of her ex. Her beautiful Janine. She of the impossible colors, hues, and shades of lovely Fran never thought she would get to have in her life. Not she, the gawky artist Frances whom nobody, not even her mom or brother and most certainly not her dad, may he rest in peace, thinks makes any sense at all. How she had won Janine, Fran never knew; with only her enigmatic oil pastels and watercolors to speak for her, lined up on the sidewalk in front of the park, beckoning passersby to adore them as she adores them.

Somehow Janine had done that—adored one of Fran's bluest blues, a fluid abstract of azure and aqua—one autumn day as the sun mellowed and Fran, warmed by its shadows, smiled at the smiling Janine. She offered up this blaze of blue to Janine for just a coffee and a chat. And Janine, leaning over her cup of joe, cradled the artwork in her arms and asked Fran about its colors.

Instantly, Fran loved her for that; she loves her still.

Loves her and all the perfect colors she and Janine saw together, hundreds of colors stretching over two years, each one more spectacular than the one before. Colors that flickered in Janine's brown eyes—she named those Janine to the first power—colors that warmed every dip and curve of Janine's body—Janine to the third, the fifth, the tenth—the color that fluttered through Janine's flaxen hair—*Palomino*—Janine to the eighth power.

Palomino. God what a beautiful color, Fran thinks again in the lonely apartment. A perfect color like that on that perfect day they had together when Janine had thrown up her hands and demanded that they go somewhere. And they had. Fran shut her box of colors and left her closet studio, and they went to the lake and rode palomino horses at sunset. Cantered along the shore, the foam of gently crashing waves mirroring the horses' sweat. Her and Janine's breath rocking back and forth, back and forth like whitecaps. A perfect day. Sky the color of bluebonnets, water the color of copper. And the palominos, their caramel sinews and flaxen manes bouncing and flying like Janine's own golden hair, whipping through the air like brushstrokes of shadow and light.

Shadow and light.

Shadow and light.

Fran had to capture that when they came home: the shadow and light of Janine.

She shut herself up in her studio again and tried to recreate the exquisite perfection of that great day together while Janine clattered dishes in the sink.

But when Fran emerged with the perfect colors of that perfect day—she had captured it finally, the glory of that exquisite day—and ached to give it to Janine, Janine didn't understand. *How could she not?*

"It's beautiful, Fran." Janine pressed her lips into a thin pink line. "Everything you create is beautiful, of course, but not everyone lives for colors the way you do, sweetie. Some of us live for people. You know, company. Companionship. Conversation."

Companionship? You are my whole companion, my love, Fran thought.

"And security, babe," Janine said. "Some of us love keeping the lights on, the rent paid, food in our bellies day after day, Fran. Some of us get tired of paying all the bills all the time while somebody works on their art. Color is sweet, honey. It's the moment. It's *now*, like you, but some of us also love tomorrow as much as today."

Now, on this December day, Fran picks up the card from Janine again, the dollar bill in the foreground beseeching her.

"Some of us also love tomorrow as much as today," Janine said that day, and for the umpteenth time she begged Fran to take the insurance job Fran's brother was offering, promising that Fran could work from home, anything to bring home dollars like Janine did day after day from the café, the coins from her tips clanking into the Mason jar they used to collect spare change. "Do it for me, please," Janine implored, and she wedged her last dollar bill into the jar. *A peace offering, a taunt, a dare? One last chance to make it right?*

This can't be happening, Fran thought.

"The beloved fears and hates the lover," Fran read once in a book, a little thin book about a tall, cross-eyed woman named Miss Amelia in love with a hunchback called Cousin Lymon. "For the lover is forever trying to strip bare his beloved," she remembers the book saying.

"For the lover is forever trying to strip bare his beloved," Fran repeats out loud. And suddenly, she understands why Janine sent the holiday card, its dollar bill fluttering seductively on the cover.

Yes, one last chance to make it right.

She reaches for the Mason jar and pulls out the lone dollar bill Janine left inside. Fran closes her eyes and presses the dollar between her palms. An American dollar. A masterpiece universally adored.

"Janine adores you," Fran whispers. "My perfect Janine adores this perfect masterpiece."

And she rushes again to her art table in the closet. Fran pins the dollar to the acid-free paper on her table and peers at the dollar's design.

Next to her lies her art case, a large three-tiered wooden box lavishly carved—sea serpents, mermaids, and Neptune there looking as if he were alive. Fran strokes the box, tracing the rise and fall of the figures the way she does when colors come to her and she has to catch them, right then, lest they float away and be gone, beyond her grasp the way Janine was gone. Beyond her grasp.

Fran opens the box.

She lowers her magnifying glass and clicks on her drafting light. Its warmth washes over her rows and rows of pens and pastels and watercolors, all shapes and sizes—wide-swathed, hair-thin, blunt-tipped. Ash gray. Pine green. Sage. She breathes in. Burnt Sienna.

Bamboo. Cacao. Raw Pumpkin. She strokes the colors. Green Apple. Burlap. Labrador Black, Toffee, Teal, Clamshell, and her beloved Palomino.

Oh, those are some sweet, sweet colors. Going, going, gone, she thinks. *Goodbye, sweet colors. Time for the gray-flannel suit.* The work-a-day-world she had so long avoided. The colorless world that Fran's brother's offer still promises. "Just give it a chance, sis. People need insurance as much as art," he said, and Janine, listening, put her hands together and pleaded with her to take it. *Oh Janine,* Fran thinks and all the small blue veins in her body ache.

She looks down at the humble dollar bill pinned to her draft board. "Everybody loves you, my friend," she says, running her fingers over it again. "You are universally adored."

And with that she angles the light closer and studies the dollar's gradations of shading.

"Yankee greenback, you've got some sweet colors too."

And she sets to work, sketching out the contours of the bill, penciling in the circles and rectangles and arcs before drawing George Washington himself. Slowly, Fran recreates the tiny gray-green cross hatches beneath Washington's chin, and there again on the side of his face, in the ruffle of his shirt, the fold of his collar. *Now that's gravitas,* she thinks. *George was nobody's fool,* Fran says to herself as she draws, replicating the arch of his eyebrow, the dimple in his chin, the purse of his lips.

"Oh George," she sighs, "Bring her back to me."

For hours she works, feathering the leaves in each corner, the number "one" encased in a swirling oval, another in an oblong shield, two more in near circles below, across a field of pale gray-green paper faded, faded to what? What shade is that, Fran thinks, this albino split pea green? The lush colors in her art box call to her but she soldiers on.

"THE UNITED STATES OF AMERICA, she draws in delicate black ink, floating, it seems, over its shadow. "FEDERAL RESERVE NOTE" etches out from a thick line of blackness; "ONE DOLLAR" hovers, formidable, below George.

"This note is legal tender," Fran tapers each letter, "for debts, public and private."

"Damn straight," she whispers as the dawn glimmers outside and her masterpiece shines. Then, where the Secretary of the Treasury's signature should be, Fran, still hardening her heart against the other colors, signs her own name in black ink with a flourishing hand.

While the ink dries and the sun rises, she reaches under her drafting table for a padded envelope thick and soft enough to protect this finest of peace offerings yet.

To Janine, Fran writes on the envelope's back in somber black.

She stops. The intensity of the night's work comes back to her, her arms suddenly heavy, her fingers stiff as she closes her box of colors.

Fran holds her dollar in front of her, caressing the velvety sheen of its paper. She slides the dollar into an acetate sleeve and tucks it between two cardboard panels. Gently, she tapes the panels together.

One perfect dollar, she writes on the top. *A masterpiece, universally adored (like you, my love).*

Merry Christmas, she writes.

Love, Frances.

PS: I'm taking the job.

Bald Tires

"One dollar! Woo-hoo!" she shouted up the basement steps. "Honey, I found an extra dollar in your jeans' pocket. Another dollar, darlin', for the kitty. That's good news, isn't it?"

"Oh my, and look at this." She pulled a handful of coins out of another pair of jeans covered in dust from the quarry. "Another seventy-five cents in your other pants. Why this is a happy day! Seaside vacation here we come!" She slipped the dollar bill and coins into the pocket of her apron and turned back to the washing machine.

She held the rumbled dungarees in both hands, her skin reddened and rougher now than before, and looked up the stairway past the bare light bulb hanging down and waited though no reply came, only the garbled drone of Monday Night Football playing on the TV in the living room.

She turned back to the laundry and after a moment footsteps clunked across the kitchen floor above. The refrigerator door opened and closed quickly, and the cushing sound of a beer can opening wafted down the stairs.

She stopped and listened to the rattle of his key chain clipped onto his belt loop.

"Baby," she called quickly, the quiver in her voice swaddled in the sweetness she'd been known for, the sing-songy uplift he'd once adored. "Want me to make you some nachos, darlin'? I got some of that new picante sauce you like so much. Why, folks say it makes home-made nachos just as good as the ones at Los Lobos."

She twisted the ruffle of the apron she wore constantly these days it seemed, stretched tighter now across her midriff, softer and wider as it was like the other wives, the ones with babies in tow though no baby tugged at her bosom after all, cranky for want of mother's milk. She'd have been the one to do it too, nurse her baby the old-fashioned way, like their grandmas and great-grannies had done, low-class and nasty though the girls today said it was, and swore they'd rather die than sink so low. "Never you mind," she'd told the other gals before her baby'd come, then gone, so tiny and weak and early.

"Never you mind," she'd said to him as well, though in her heart she knew he hadn't been ready for either a baby or a wife or the life she'd tried to make for them and still wanted to have.

"So, how about you let me make you some of those good ole nachos?" she shouted up the steps, picking up another bundle of dirty clothes. "Why don't you just settle in for the rest of the night?

"Why, they say it's going to rain tonight anyway, and you know those tires are so bald, they're 'bout to burst. Ain't no good in the rain, honey. You said that yourself why just last week. And Lord knows, if anyone knows best 'bout cars it's you, sugar."

She held up a white t-shirt, found a spot of grease, a Big Mac dribble maybe or chicken fries, and poured extra detergent on it, rubbing it together like her mother used to.

"No sir, no good in the rain at all. Just think what a hardship it'd be having that old jalopy go crashing into one of them big oak trees down close to town. Why, where'd we be then, without a truck or money enough to fix it? I know how that pains you, darlin', having things go wrong like that. Why, you need your rest, sweetheart. You work too hard to be burdened with troubles like that. Yes sir, you deserve better, husband, much, much better than a smashed-up pick-up and being stuck out here in the middle of nowhere with just stupid old me for company."

She paused and tilted her ear toward the stairway, cradling a new bundle of dirty clothes like the sleeping child they'd never had. The television rumbled on. She lifted a dingy undershirt from the pile and breathed in its acrid odor. One-by-one she peeled clothes from the pile, checked the pockets, and tossed them into the washer: his Tennessee Titans t-shirt, the dress shirt he wore to church, plaid boxers, cotton socks, dungarees, pushing them all into the same jumbo load, whites and colors together until only his Sunday trousers were left.

"Why, if we use the kitty, we're getting close to having all the money for some brand-new tires, so you won't have to give it another thought." She pressed the trousers to her chest and waited and waited for a response that didn't come, again.

She sighed and held the pants out before her as she had the dungarees and searched the pockets one by one. A half pack of gum, a gas receipt, crumpled napkin, three pennies, one dime, a nickel, and there in the front left pocket, a bundle of dollar bills. She smiled and glanced up the stairs, holding the dollar bills in one hand, her mouth already open and ready to shout out the good news.

But then she stopped. She looked again at the folded bills and peeled them back slowly like lettuce leaves and there, nestled beneath the dollars, was a single condom, its silver foil unbroken.

She stopped, her arm bent, the crinkling packet perched inside the green bills in her hand. For a long time she looked at it, its shiny package a perfect square like a York Peppermint Patty.

Then, silently, she slid the packet back inside the bills and started to put it into her apron pocket with the other loose change for the kitty.

But then she stopped and looked around the basement, at the shelves full of paint cans and yard tools. She crossed over to a group of boxes stacked against the wall and opened one labeled *Christmas*. She dug around inside and pulled out an old Christmas cookie tin. Holding the metal box between her knees she pried the lid off and slipped the bundle of bills inside. She started to press the top back on, but then stopped and scooped the extra dollar and jumble of coins from her apron pocket and dropped them into the tin as well. The coins rattled and she quickly closed the metal box.

Glancing up the steps, she slid the cookie tin far back onto the laundry shelf behind the spot remover and fabric softener. Pausing, she flopped her bag of rags over the tin and turned back to the laundry. She scooped out a ladle of detergent and sprinkled it slowly over the wash. She turned the washer level to jumbo and pushed the hot/warm button, the machine coming alive before her, a cascade of clean, warming water rushing over his dirty clothes.

"No, siree," she said to the open washer, her voice rising ever so slightly. "Not one more worried thought 'bout them tires. A body can just drive and drive and drive without a care in the world once them tires are fixed. Now, won't that be nice? Won't that be worth all the one dollars in the world?"

Little Jimmy

"One dollar. *Pssch!*" Randy spat into the daffodils overtaking his lawn. That's all he had left from the $50 his wife had given him before she left. "For the weekend," she'd said as if he could still tell one day from the next, but Randy knew it was forever.

"Forever and a day," she used to say, "that's how long I'll love you." Back when "forever and a day" still meant getting it on every single day.

"Maybe we ought to prove 'forever' every two days, baby," he'd said then. "We got to let Little Jimmy rest. Boy's a stallion, that's true, but even thoroughbreds got to sleep."

$

His wife—though she wasn't his wife then—had slapped him on the butt. Hard. It'd hurt, but of course he couldn't let her know that. That's how it was back then in their glory days—he was invincible, and she was horny.

"God, give me back my sweet horny wife," Randy said to no one in particular, certainly not to God, to whom he hadn't spoken in what—ten, eleven years—however long it'd been since the wedding. He'd prayed that night, he remembered, a silent, half-drunk bridegroom's prayer about stamina and performance. Maybe it'd pissed God off, since things had gone decidedly downhill since then.

First, his pecker conked out on him. "Lay off the sauce, sweetheart," his wife had said. "Little Jimmy will come roaring back." But he hadn't, laid off the sauce, that is. He'd pretended to—told his wife he had, a lie like all the other lies—switched over to Absolut vodka so his breath wouldn't smell and took up eating licorice even though he couldn't stand the stuff. Nasty little black strings that made his teeth go gray like an old man's.

Once Little Jimmy quit on him, the rest had just fallen in after. Disappeared. Job, house. Hell, even his hair fell out and left him bald as a baby's bottom. *Just my luck.*

He waved a horsefly off his head. "Man's life leads where his pecker points, son," his grandfather had told him one hot summer day when, for no reason at all, his teeny weenie had risen to a full salute right there in front of his grandfather. He'd tried to hide it, Randy remembered, but his grandpa had set in laughing and slapping him on his back and laid that little pearl of wisdom on him.

And now where had his pecker led him, unreliable tool that it was? To a rusted-out lounge chair in the backyard of their foreclosed house with no job, no wife, no hair, and one lousy dollar in his pocket.

"Damn you, Jimmy," Randy said aloud and tossed the empty Absolut bottle into the oleander just before his cell phone rang and his wife's name flashed across the screen.

"God double damn you, Jimmy, you son of a bitch," Randy shouted as he looked at the phone. "Get back here and tell me what to do."

The Grass Jesus Walked On

"One dollar!" Young Earl C. Calder looked at the farmer before him transfixed on the small blue vial Earl held in his hand.

Earl didn't blink in the midday sun, all 110 pounds of himself holding steady next to Ida. The vial of elixir they had emptied the night before still floated through him, but he didn't flinch, not Madam Wilma T.'s son, born in a brothel and groomed for greatness.

"One dollar," he said again and tapped the inky blue container. "This here blade of grass is the real thing, friend. Walked on by the Savior himself, Jesus Christ, the Son of God, one thousand eight hundred and sixty-six years ago on his way to the cross."

Beside him young Ida C. Morrow leaned her lithe body forward, holding out a weathered moccasin they'd found in the peddler's belongings and patting its underside. "Sanctified," she said in her soft New Orleanian murmur, "by the sole of He who died for our sins."

She tilted her head down and smiled sweetly the way Madam Wilma had insisted the girls do at the brothel, especially the new ones fresh from their stations in the kitchen or laundry or sewing circles where they earned their keep until they reached their age of consent, a whole thirteen years of age in New Orleans according to the Napoleonic Code in 1866. "Sweetness, girls. Sweetness sells," the Madam would say. "Sweetness brings Papa Bear to the honey pot, and you, my sweets, are the sweetest honey pots in all of Orleans Parish."

Ida closed her eyes and shook her head. She steadied herself at the edge of the wagon. Her dark curls bounced, and a stray strand plastered itself in the sweat along her pale pink temple. *Sweetness,* she thought, and suddenly she felt sick again, sick like she'd felt the whole of her twelfth year watching her thirteenth birthday grow closer and closer.

The elixir she'd drunk with Earl the night before welled up in her and Ida forced a swallow. She hadn't wanted any of it in Madam Wilma's employ, not the long hours in the kitchen ducking Cook's ire, not the leers of the rich old men who came to the brothel waiting, waiting for the youngest girls to ripen into service, and most especially she hadn't wanted the fawning, liquor-laced embrace of the displaced old mayor, desperate to salvage his Southern manhood on the tiny bodies of Wilma T.'s youngest conscripts.

"Yes sir, touched by the Savior's soul!" Earl's sing-songy refrain filtered through to Ida, and she smiled again, sweetly. The farmer and his lanky son were leaning in to Earl now, ogling the blue vial he cupped in his hand, their curiosity ablaze. The blue of the bottle and the blue of Earl's eyes danced before her.

She had wanted Earl, though, this pretty-faced young man with the easy laugh and boyish swagger that had charmed his mother so. "Born to lead," the Madam had sworn, and for a quick flash Ida wondered if she were dreaming that he'd really gone and done it, broken free of his mama at last, broken the hold she had on both of them.

They had fled, snuck out of the brothel in the wee hours when the errant husbands and preachers and foreign sailing men had crept back to their wives and parsonages and vessels, the fire of their manhood tamed for one more night. Even the piano player had gone to bed when Earl and Ida had slipped out the kitchen door, their meager possessions stuffed in an old satchel, and skittered down the empty cobblestones to the edge of the opium district, where they'd run across the peddler lying doped up and snoring outside a Chinese laundry.

Taking the wagon had been Ida's idea, and Earl had heartily agreed. "Why, it's the perfect means of transport and disguise," he'd said, and they'd scratched a Bill of Sale on the back of a flea powder label that had fallen off one of the peddler's wares.

"Sold," Ida had pronounced and stuffed a handful of Confederate dollars into the sleeping peddler's coat pocket, the worthless coin of rebellion, and off they'd gone, headed to Texas and a life unknown.

Bending over the edge of that wagon, Earl C. Calder spoke in a gruff whisper. Ida strained to hear his proclamation to the farmer.

"Just one dollar, sir, for a piece of the sacred ground walked on by our Lord himself, yours to have and to hold here in Port Neches and wash away the sins of our souls." Earl waved the blue vial again before the grizzled face of the farmer, the wet spring mud of East Texas caked across his overalls.

"Young sins, brother." Earl lowered his voice like Ida's murmur. "Yours and mine and Ida's here. Sins of the father and sins of the son. Young or old as we are, we all have sins, mister." Earl knelt and placed his hand on the shoulder of the farmer's tall, scrawny son standing wide-eyed and smitten before Ida.

"Sold," said the farmer, and from somewhere deep in the pockets of his dungarees still stained with Confederate defeat, the farmer grabbed hold of a Yankee dollar, the wretched coin of capitulation, and gave it over to Ida perched between the boxes of elixirs and broadcloth and cast-iron kettles that had once been the stock in trade of a Connecticut peddler.

"Bless you, sir." Ida smiled kindly again and plunked the man's Union coin into the pocket of her muslin skirt, frayed at the hemline and flecked with grass stains. She took the small blue vial from Earl's fingers and handed it to the farmer. "May it bring you a lifetime of blessings from our Lord and Savior, Jesus Christ," she said. "The one and only Son of God."

The farmer took the small bottle in his rough hands and brought it to his lips. "Thank you, lassie," he muttered, and laying his hand on the shoulder of the boy beside him, turned to go.

"Sir," Ida suddenly called to him, but the farmer, unaccustomed perchance to being addressed as such, didn't turn. "Brother Believer," Ida called again and this time the man stopped and turned, and Ida scampered down from atop the peddler's wagon holding something.

"As a show of our appreciation, sir, we give you this switch dipped in the River Jordan by John the Baptist himself." Ida reached out to hand the man a long, slim twig stripped of leaves.

"Lest any wickedness descends upon your only son here," Earl added, rushing over to Ida's side, "as he wades into the perilous waters of manhood."

The farmer, startled perhaps by such magnanimity, stepped forward, took the switch, and lowered it to his side. "Thank you kindly, young'uns." He looked from Earl to Ida. "Ways of the world's a troublesome road, that's a true born fact."

And with that, the farmer laid his arm back across his son's back and the two of them strode off toward the mule-drawn wooden wagon beside the Opelousas Trail folks traveled on in these parts, cattlemen and preachers and immigrant folk, the same rough road Generalissimo López de Santa Anna had once walked on, shackled and chained by triumphant Texans on a long walk of shame to New Orleans.

Earl turned and winked at Ida, who smiled and wiped away the Texas sweat on her brow. She lifted the hem of her skirt out of the dust and turned back to the wagon. Earl held out his hand, and Ida took it as she stepped back up onto the wagon's seat.

Gently, Ida ran her hand over the leaflet that a drunk and defeated Confederate soldier, the right side of his body mangled, had left at the brothel, taking advantage of the Madam's soft spot for the fallen South. Ida had stuffed it in her apron pocket and shown it to Earl, and he had grinned and kissed Ida on the lips the way he'd done only once before, and Ida had blushed and Earl had blushed. And right then and there they'd sealed the deal of running off together.

They'd tacked the leaflet inside the peddler's wagon as soon as they headed out of New Orleans. *Great is Texas,* read the pamphlet. *"Great! Grand! Glorious! Ranchers Paradise, Cheap Land – Low Taxes!"*

"Tell me again," Ida turned to Earl, this sweet-faced boy into whose hands she'd thrown her whole lot in life, "how we're gonna turn the Devil's Desert into God's Green Earth."

Earl walked over to the blue beard grass growing on the side of the dirt road they'd traveled miles beyond the Louisiana line. He reached down and pulled another tuft of the long blue blades out of the ground.

"Why, it's just like what we just did with these here blades of grass, Ida," Earl said. "We took a piece of some-thing worthless. Something stepped on every day by the poor saps coming and going from the burdensome business of life, and we turned it into something grand, like the paper says. 'Great and grand and glorious', just like Texas.

"Praise the Lord!" Earl continued, plucking the blades of beard grass one by one from the cluster and wiping them off on the belly of his shirt. "This here's our gold mine, Ida." He picked up an empty blue vial from the box next to Ida and threaded a new single blade of beard grass gently inside and popped the cork back on.

"Why, it's just like God's work, Ida." Earl held the bottle before him. "We'll just feed the faithful in the promised land. And what's the harm in that?"

"Guess God ain't gonna smite us dead like I first thought he would," she laughed, pulling the farmer's dollar coin out of her pocket and plopping it into the rusted tobacco tin hidden beneath the bins of thimbles and boxes of nails.

"You know, giving that farmer that switch of dogwood, the one—what did you call it? —the one 'Dipped in the River Jordan by John the Baptist himself.' That was a stroke of pure genius, Ida," Earl said. "And a real nice gesture, too, 'specially coming from a gal as sweet as you. We gotta keep that in." He looked deep into Ida's dark brown eyes.

Ida laughed and felt again a warmth sweep over her like the balm of the elixir, and she suddenly didn't regret any of it, not the leaving, nor the stealing, nor the trickery that was all they had to save themselves in the great wild land of Texas.

"Why, thank you, Earl," she laughed. "I do think it was well worth that farmer's dollar."

Grocery List

"One dollar off frozen string beans. That'll work. Fifty cents off peanut butter; we can do chunky—the kids'll eat it even if he won't. Seventy-five cents off mac and cheese—I know it's crap but it's cheap and filling. Oh look, I have three of those. Yippee! OK, let me check the sales. I could take the 70 bus down to the Safeway if they're not on sale at Giant. Oh wait, bus fare. Shit, have to add that in. Rats. Oh well, I can walk, got my cart. Good for me anyway, work off some of this big butt he's always fussing about. Yeah, you used to like it, buster, cushion for the ride, you said. Oh well, screw that anyway, you're never home. Just as well. Good riddance I say, Jesus, what a grouch. Take the damn job, why don't you. It ain't fuckin' beneath you. Going hungry is beneath all of us, most especially Robbie who's only three for Christ's sake. How the hell is he supposed to understand your ridiculous pride? Oh, there's an opening in the kitchen at his school, did I tell you? Put in for it yesterday, will hear on Monday. Got my sister praying for me, I don't care how much you hate that. Shit, it can't hurt for heaven's sake, it's only words and she loves to do that. OK, so that's $3.75 in coupons plus whatever the sales save. Make it an even $5. This week's economy goal! Not bad. Well done, Mom. You rock. Yeah, that's right. I rock. Save a nickel, save a dime, save a goddamn dollar one day at a time."

Van Camp's Pork & Beans

One dollar. That's all the little thing would have cost. Flashes like her mother's rage began to flicker inside of her. *It was right there at the check-out counter, next to the bug spray and Chapstick, last-minute items campers forget. That's why they're there—because people <u>forget</u>.*

"Don't worry, we've got one," her boyfriend had said. "Not to worry, babe, your old buddy boy here has got it covered."

"I know, sweetheart." She'd kept her voice even, the way she'd practiced, "But let's get another one just in case."

"No need, ducky wucky. Who's the gear guy here?" He grinned. "Grizzly Adams or Little Bo Peep?"

"I'm just saying," she countered. *Calm, stay calm,* she told herself. "That it'd be a helluva thing to forget, out here in the boonies, honey, where it's just you and me and the bears." She smiled at him, her pooky bear. "It won't hurt to get another, just to be sure. You know how I like to be sure. Please? It'll help me sleep."

"Oh, don't worry, pumpkin. Out here, wrapped in these hairy-beary arms, you'll sleep like a kitten." He wrapped his arms around her then and lifted her two feet off the ground.

The clerk, Irene her nametag said, laughed when he did that and called him a one-of-a-kind kind of guy and shook her head. "The Lord done broke the mold when He made you, mister." Irene clucked a hot cocoa kind of cluck and rung up the rest of their supplies.

Take a breath, she'd told herself, and she had looked out at the tall pine trees on the hillside outside, swaying in the breeze, tisk-tisking their needly fingers at her, warning her not to take his word for it, not to let his big man's pride, brittle as a dry leaf, dissuade her again.

"Oh, all right," she relented, relaxing her jaw like the therapist said and letting her agitation dissolve. "What's the worst that could happen?" she asked Irene and wriggled loose from his brawny, tawny arms and thumped him on the biceps. "Old Popeye arms here would have to squeeze these open with his big bare hands."

She grabbed two cans of Van Camp's Pork and Beans and held them high like barbells and everyone had laughed, his hurly burly big-man pride safe once more from woman-scorn, she called it, the acid words her mother'd rained upon her head when she was small and full of fear, words of scorn she swore she'd never say nor let be said to her again.

And now, hours later, here they were, out on big Green Mountain, just the two of them and all their cans of pork and beans. Her stomach growled and again the angry words rumbled, but she bit her tongue and tossed him a can of Van Camp's like he'd asked, and he laughed that deep teddy bear laugh that swept her up in its embrace.

She listened to the rapids rush beneath them, here on the sunny side of the mountain, sunlight glinting off the pines one year to the day of their first day together. She watched him, her pooky bear, as quietly, can in hand, he began to search for it, that dollar thing they had not bought, sifting through granola bars, checking all his pockets, slowly unpacking, repacking all their gear until finally he turned to her, his ducky wucky gal.

"Well, I'll be damned." He grinned his old boyish grin. "Looks like Papa Bear forgot the can opener after all, beautiful."

She sighed, that barely audible sigh that had enraged her mother so, setting off a torrent of insults: *ugly, fat, and stupid; the perfect imperfection of a daughter; born to be a burden, born to be alone.*

Breathe in, she told herself, and she breathed in the cool pine air. "Breathe out," she whispered, and, rising slowly from her perch beside the fire, she ran her long thin fingers over shards of bark and needles turned to brown, and there, beneath the pine cones she found a shaft of shale.

"Try this, sweetheart," she called to him, her voice steady and calm, and tossed him the slivered shale.

"Oh perfect, darlin'," he hurrahed, and grabbed a stone from off the ground; with the Van Camp's tight between his knees, he slowly chiseled open their pork and beans.

"Look at it this way," she wrapped her arms around her pooky bear as the beans warmed on the fire, "At least we saved a dollar."

Magic Fingers

One dollar for a jiggle, a jostle, a shake.

"Put four quarters in the slot, miss," the motel clerk had said, the burn scar on his top lip stretched into a smile, "and let the Magic Fingers ease all your troubles away. You won't find this in any of your fancy New York hotels, I can tell you that."

Paulina handed the laminated photo of the room back to him and peeled twenty bucks off her roll of tips from the Ladies Room at the Ritz Carlton.

"Great," she'd given him her best lopsided smile, careful not to show the broken tooth there on the left side of her mouth. "What's another dollar?" She waved her pale, weary hand with the same merciless disdain of her customers tossing a stray bill into the tip basket strategically placed beside the door of the marble-floored Ladies Room. For the past twenty-one months she had hidden there from him, silencing the terror in her heart with a lilting cheeriness. "Care for a towel, Madame?"

What did they know, though, these ladies of the auxiliary clubs, of the meaning—the true value—of a dollar?

"You won't regret it, miss," the night clerk with the disfigured brown face had smiled, and she'd smiled back at him, a closed-lipped, earnest, midnight-in-nowhere smile, one damaged soul to another.

And she hadn't regretted it. She'd lain face down on the faded purple bedspread with the port wine stain on the edge, plunked four quarters into the box of the Magic Fingers, and drifted. She dreamed that she was Dorothy, spinning, spinning far, far away where he could never find her, Toto by her side and Glenda, the Good Witch of the North, looking after her.

"Hey!" A woman's voice came to her. *The Wicked Witch of the West*, she thought. *Oh God, she's found me.*

"H-e-e-e-y!"

Paulina, face down on the bed, scrambled to sit up.

"H-e-e-e-y. You in there!" The woman was drunk. Her tongue floated in the back of her throat.

"Come on, darlin'," a man's voice interrupted. He was drunk too, but happy drunk, got-him-a-woman-and-I'm-gonna-get-laid drunk.

Paulina waited. Drunk she knew. Drunk she could handle. And happy drunk? *Pff!* That was a walk in the park. Not like him, her ex, a volcanic drunk he was, breathing fire over the phone at the Ritz Carlton once he'd tracked her down, violating the sanctity of her Ladies Room, and gotten her fired.

"You understand, Paulina," her boss had said. "A place like this, we just can't have any trouble."

"H-e-e-e-y!" The woman was beating the door with her palm. "You got a dollar? I want me some Magic Fingers and I ain't got a dime."

Paulina stifled a laugh. What the hell did she have to laugh about, holed up in a seedy motel outside of Pittsburgh with a crazy drunk woman at the door?

"Pu-u-l-e-e-e-z!" the woman pleaded, and, despite her better judgment, despite everything she knew about drunks and strangers and trouble, Paulina reached into her handbag and, creeping on all fours, slid four shiny quarters under the door.

"O-o-o-h, thank you-u-u!" gurgled the woman. "God is gonna bless you, bless you, bless you! Bless all the days of your life," she shouted, and the man giggled like a girl.

"You got us a dollar, sugar," he said. "Magic Fingers, here we come!"

Paulina crawled back to the bed and, leaning over it like she had as a child, she put her hands together. "Dear God," she said, "please bless me, bless me, bless me, for all the days of my life. Amen."

Parents and Children

Primin' the Pump

"One dollar? Is that enough? Who are you kidding, son? No way! One lousy dollar all by itself in a sax case? That's pathetic. Ain't nobody gonna get inspired by that. Shit. You ain't worth a damn dollar if that's all you got. You got to prime the pump, boy, put at least five bucks there, plus a fist full of change. Quarters—make 'em quarters. None of this nickel shit. Damn nickels, ain't worth the time it takes a tall man to bend over and pick them up. You got to give folks something to *aspire to*. It's all about *aspiration*, son."
"Go on, put some out there."

"All right now—that's more like it. What's that? Six bucks and change? Good. Good. Wait a minute—these babies are damn near brand new. Shit, where you been, boys? This ain't the ATM. Crinkle them up. These babies got to look used, worn out, like they been living in wallets for years, stuffed down into pockets and shit, and you have *inspired* someone to take them out and give them *away*."

"No, no, no, that's not it. Here—lemme show you. Turn some of them green side up, some green, some gray—make it look random, you know, like they just fell that way. All right, put some of them quarters on top, sprinkle them over there. Maybe a few dimes, make it look believable, you know."

"Well, let's see—stand tall, y'all—how's it look? Yeah, that's better—a veritable bouquet of money just begging for company. OK, y'all? First train's coming in—you all tuned up? No? Well, get on it, fellas, hurry up. Come on now. Train's coming in. See the light? Your B flat's off, son, sharpen it up. Come on now: *do re me fa so la ti do ... do ... do...do ... Do it! Good! Do ti la so fa me re do-o-o-o-o.*"

"Aspiration!"

"*All right!* It's show time, gentlemen! Gimme one of Saint John's *Favorite Things*, which, God help us, never was, never will be, one of them lousy dollars. May Saint John forgive us."

"Five, six, seven, eight ..."

Cargo Pants

One dollar. One dollar. OK, OK, that's all I need, Davey thought, his eleven-year-old brain scrambling to make this new problem not a problem, not an emergency, not another humiliating mistake he had to call his mom about, and how would he do that anyway without any money?

He could handle this. He'd found his way to the Metro station, hadn't he, even when the bus driver wouldn't let him on.

"Sorry kid," the driver had said, "It's my first day on the job, so I've gotta follow the rules. Your monthly pass expired yesterday, buddy. I can't let you on. Sorry."

Sure, Davey'd been scared at first, this had never happened before, then he was pissed at his mom for not remembering to get him a new pass—she was usually on top of stuff like that—but then, he'd remembered that he knew the way, at least the way the bus went from his school to the Metro, so he could just follow the route, and that's what he'd done. Walked the bus route all the way even though it was kinda cold outside, and now here he was, safe at the Metro. *Was that cool or what? Alright!* He was one smart kid. Yeah OK, he was late, his mom would be pissed, but he was late a lot and she always got over it, and besides, wasn't it kind of her fault anyway?

But now, *crap,* he'd even lost his stupid dollar, the one he hadn't spent on lunch the way he was supposed to, the one he was gonna use to buy a jumbo Reese's Peanut Butter Cup instead, but now, *GA-A-A-A,* even that was gone and how the hell was he going to buy a farecard?

Again, he searched his pockets, the ones in back without the holes and the ones in front with the holes that he'd forgotten about—again—that had loosed his dollar into the world—again. *Stupid pants, why'd they have to have holes in them?* Why hadn't he asked his mom to fix them and didn't she check his pockets all the time anyway, so why hadn't she seen the holes and fixed them already?

"One dollar," Davey said aloud this time, loud enough for the people crowding around the farecard machine to hear. "One dollar, one dollar." He pulled his empty pockets inside out this time, but all he found were the stupid pebbles they'd been throwing on top of the sports shed at school before the security guard caught them and made them stop.

"Don't make me have to tell Mr. Pope, now, boys," she had said. "You knuckleheads stop this nonsense now, you hear?"

Come on, come on. His stomach was starting to clench up. *There's gotta be a dollar somewhere in one of these stupid pockets.*

The line in front of the farecard machine was getting longer. An old lady in a blue coat looked down at him. She had that look his mother had when he pretended to be asleep but really was just faking it so he could skip social studies class first period with Miz what's her name, who made them copy the entire glossary from the back of the book like it was real learning and not just some stupid busy work even his dad thought was crap.

"One dollar," he said again under his breath, peeking at the lady in the blue coat from behind his shaggy white boy hair. This time he checked the side pockets of his cargo pants, the ones that hung low beneath his knees, too big for his small frame his mom said, they were bigger than he was. "What're you gonna hide in there, buddy, a bottle of vodka or a few Molotov cocktails?" she had asked, sarcastic like she always was. He didn't know what a Molotov cocktail was but he sure as hell wasn't gonna let his mother know that, not her who was against this plan all along: against him taking the subway home alone all across town every day without so much as a beeper to keep in touch.

"One dollar, one dollar, one dollar, one dollar, one dollar," he muttered, his words echoing in his chest, once for each pocket, once for each month before his twelfth birthday, once for each time he'd promised his mom he'd come right home after school. "One dollar," came a final echo. Davey looked up. The lady in the blue coat was still staring at him, a crisp dollar bill in her hand.

"Looks like you could use this, young man." She smiled that same grandma smile his neighbor had when she caught him up top the tallest tree on the block, the same smile his mom would have, he was sure, after he told her what all had happened, the same smile his heart was having right now looking up at this nice lady.

"Oh, yes ma'am," he said even though he never said "ma'am." *Oh man, where did that come from,* he thought, and suddenly, before he could stop it, before he could get his game face on, that little-happy-kid-grin he hated so much, that old ladies and especially his mom liked so much burst across his face. "Yes, ma'am," he said again and so help him, he didn't even care this time if he sounded like a dork. "One dollar's all I need."

The Bell

$1.00. The yard sale tag on the old bell wasn't sticking to the brass due to all the rust laced across it, so I rubbed my fingernail back and forth into the white sticker, hoping some small bit of stickum would attach.

Somebody needs to take this. There is too much history here to bear.

The bell had been my Yankee mother Abigail's. "Abby. Like in Westminster," she used to tell people when they first met. "Only I'm more like an ancient ruin rotting in Texas without air conditioning." I always laughed at this, my mother's one repetitive joke, though, truth be told, I never thought it was very funny.

My mother was lonely. Deeply lonely in a way nobody around her understood, me included. It was something I'd come to understand about my mother's life only after it was too late.

I turned the bell over, careful to hold the pendulum still lest it clang and the whole of my childhood come clamoring back.

My mama had lived in a big house with a husband and children and a dog or three and one lost cat over the years, but she had remained excruciatingly alone, a lone Yankee white woman with integrationist ideas in a sea of segregated Southerners.

So, every night, she'd called her children home to supper.

With her bell, the big dinner bell that my dad, Allen, had mounted outside in the backyard. When supper was ready my mother would tug at its string until its *Clang! Clang! Clang!* rose above the sounds of the crickets and the wind.

Before, my mother, Abigail, used to go outside and shout—"Peggy! Becky! Bobby!"—but her voice would narrow to a shrill warble, and so the bell was bought.

Abby's shouting days were over.

Her children grew, and our wanderings soon took us beyond the call of the bell. Our mother'd waited. She was lonely, but we children loved her, and so we always came home.

"I always came home," I said suddenly aloud.

I turned toward the cluster of small-town folk rummaging through the yard sale my father'd begged me to have after the coroner cleared the death certificate. *Natural causes, heart failure,* he'd declared, and my father had wept. I'd wept too, wept for all the years I'd been gone and left my mother behind dying slowly.

"I'm here now, Mama," I said softly.

"What are these things, honey?" a sunburnt lady in a Houston Oilers t-shirt asked.

"Oh, those would be bridge trays, ma'am," I told her. "You put your teacup there and your finger sandwiches there, nice and ladylike, see?"

"Well, I'll be. Right nice now, isn't it, sugar." The lady handed me two weathered dollar bills. "Now just got to learn me some bridge like them ladies-club gals," the woman laughed.

"I'm sure you'll do fine," I laughed with her. "Just start reading the bridge column in the *Galveston Daily News*, ma'am. My mama read that thing religiously, and she was one mean bridge player."

My mother had been one mean bridge player. She'd tried many times to coax my sister and me into playing with her and our dad, but neither of us ever took to it like our mama had. All strategy and poker-face, my mother Abby was, never letting her opponents see the desperation in her heart.

Why didn't you fight more, Mama? Like the master strategist you were. Maybe you would have if you'd kept shouting.

But time passed. We children wandered farther and came home less often. Mama stopped making supper and took to her bed. She drank clear, hard liquor and began to shout again—"Allen! Allen! Allen!"

My father had brought in the bell that sat rusting on the fence outside. I traced the line of decay running along its rim. He'd cleaned it and polished it and given it to his wife again, and this time she'd tugged at its string until its *Clang! Clang! Clang!* rose above the sound of the clear, hard liquor sitting beside her, shouting. Its voice soon rose above the clanging of the bell.

Abby's voice faded into a single thin cry of pain, and she passed on.

$

Across the yard near the hedge separating my mother's house from the neighbor's, two freckled sisters tussled over the black pillbox hat with its cluster of shimmering feathers that my mother used to wear to funerals. My sister had worn it at our mother's memorial, tucking her own long hair up into a French twist in tribute to our mama.

"Saw it first, you," said the older girl, slapping the hat on her head backwards.

"Well butter my butt and call me a biscuit, don't you look precious!" her younger sister laughed.

"Do not!"

"Do too!" said the younger girl.

"Oh, shut your sorry ass mouth!" The older girl snatched the hat off her head and slapped it back down on the card table. "Don't need no church lady hat no how."

I closed my eyes and let the musky smell of coming rain wash over me. The yard sale was winding down, the purging of the detritus of family life dribbled out to strangers driving down the wide streets of my hometown, quieter now and lonelier still since the plants closed.

I held the bell out before me in my bony, pale hand and tugged hard at its string, and it let out a solidary *clang*, crisp and loud like it always had.

A long blue sedan driving down the road suddenly braked and pulled into the driveway sideways.

"Oh baby, I got to get me that there," the woman driving the car shouted as she flung open the door. She strode over to me and took the bell in both her hands. Three light-skinned children peered out of the car windows.

"I'm 'bout to bust a vein hollering at these damn fool children with their earphones on all the time to get out the street and get their butts back in the house and eat this supper I done spent my hard-earned money buying and cooking up for you wild young'uns!" The woman peered back over her shoulder and waved the bell at them. "Mama gonna rock it old school now, y'all," she shouted.

I laughed, grateful for the fire of the woman's ways.

"How much you want for this thing, honey?" she asked, and before the woman could look down at the bell, I reached out and peeled off the $1.00 sticker that didn't want to stay stuck on anyway.

"Nada," I said. "For you, ma'am, it's a gift. My mother would absolutely have wanted you to have this, one old-school mama to another. Use it in good health, ma'am, and keep your children safe."

And the woman, smiling a wide-mouthed smile, laughed, and wrapped her mama arms around me. "Your mama raised a real good daughter, baby," she said. "You thank her for me, wherever she is."

And with that, she turned and clanged the bell three times. The children skittered off the windows and back inside the car, and their mama drove them all away.

Ricky Steiner Was Supposed to Die In Prison

One dollar for a Sunday paper had always seemed kinda high to folks. But not the day that story broke.

Not for Ricky Steiner anyway.

Ricky Steiner was supposed to die in prison. Slowly. Painfully. The years limping by like an arthritic old dog nobody bothered to put down.

Ricky knew that and had stopped counting the days, the way as a kid he'd stopped counting the days 'til Armageddon. Nevermind what the preacher said. It would get here when it gets here, Ricky figured, and there wasn't nothing he could do about it no how.

'Cause Armageddon, Ricky Steiner had come to understand, was just another word for life without parole.

So, he'd set to thinking about his socks. And keeping his fingernails clean. And combing what was left of his hair straight back so his daughter could admire his widow's peak the way she had as a child when he'd let her braid his long dark hair and stick pink ribbons in it like she did to her dolls back then.

"Daddy," she'd asked him that morning at the courthouse when the sentencing was done, "Can you still come and see me dance?"

"Daddy," she'd asked him every year for fifteen years, "Will I ever get to hug you again?"

She'd never let herself fully understand the way he had.

Armageddon, for a lonesome daughter, was just another word for daddy being gone.

"Daddy," his little girl had said one day, her grown-up eyes looking into his. "Daddy," she'd said, "I think that there's a way." And she'd held up the Sunday paper and pointed to the story she'd underlined.

And Ricky Steiner, who'd never much cared to read, had fixed his rheumy eyes on the page and read the notice that would change his life.

Wanted, it said, *innocent inmates wrongly convicted of crimes upstate.*

And so it had begun, this slow slog out of hell and the jaws of Armageddon.

The lawyers, skinny, young white boys mostly, had filed in one by one, letting the old big city counselor with the pure white hair sit down and start to talk. And ask the questions—all the questions—once again.

"Where were you the night your boss died?" The old lawyer had looked at Ricky from over the top of his glasses.

"What time did you quit work?"

"Where'd you go, with whom and why?" The old lawyer, sitting back in his chair, had waved his hand at the skinny fellow taking notes on a long, yellow legal pad.

And finally, would he be so kind as to open his mouth and let them take a cheek swab for the first and only time.

Ricky Steiner'd done that.

And then he'd set to counting, once again, the days and weeks and hours more of waiting as judges poured over evidence and DNA.

And Armageddon turned into just another word for hope on layaway.

Yep. One dollar for a Sunday paper had always seemed kinda high to folks. But not to Ricky Steiner and his baby girl that Armageddon-defying morning when he'd finally walked free. She'd held high the Sunday headline then, announcing her daddy's release and hugged him close, at last.

Mouse Socks

One dollar for a pair of socks. That's what the lady in the plastic vest with the blue and yellow fringe told Daisy's mother. "Really?" her mother replied. "Huh." She cocked her head and thought for a minute, then leaned over and whispered in Daisy's ear with the gravity of one spy to another. "You can pick out any pair you want, Sweet Pea, no questions asked."

No questions asked. That was the clincher for Daisy. Had she heard right? Usually, her mom had all kinds of questions challenging anything Daisy wanted to buy on their once-a-month sojourn to the big box store when her mama got paid. "Don't you think that t-shirt will swallow you? Isn't that lunchbox too girly for a sporty girl like you? Wouldn't you rather have a juicy pear than that nasty bag of Cheese Doodles?"

On and on with the twenty questions, every one of them aimed at undermining what Daisy wanted, inching her closer and closer toward what her mother insisted was cheaper or more practical or healthier, what would last and what was a piece of junk that would tear apart at the tiniest pressure. It was an endless loop that Daisy and her mother repeated every shopping trip like two-player pianos stuck on a single refrain. Daisy had gotten used to it. This was her life.

But today, today was different. "No questions asked," her mother had said, and then stepped back and put both hands in the air like it was a stick-up and Daisy was the robber. *Uh-oh. What's wrong?* Daisy thought. "I promise, whatever pair you want, Champ. It's your decision," her mother repeated.

Daisy grinned even though she knew better. *Is this some kind of trick?* she thought. She didn't want to be disappointed again. That always felt like a punch in the belly, it hurt so much. But "any pair you want," her mother had said. OK, if this was a trick, so be it. She would play along.

Daisy stepped onto the rung under the display table and dug her hands deep into the mountain of socks— long ones that went up to your knees, short ones, skinny ones, thick ones. Socks galore, all soft and velvety like kittens, each with its own cuter-than-cute animal or dancing polka dots or favorite party food woven into the design.

It was mesmerizing.

How could she possibly choose? How does a girl even make a choice? What does that feel like? The mounds of socks loomed larger and more ominous. *I need to pick something small,* she thought. *Something little and harmless and cute.* She tossed aside the dinosaurs, the galaxies far, far away, the lions and tigers and bears.

"Oh my," she muttered.

Even the whales and porpoises were too daunting. And the pizza and ice cream cone and candy cane socks were just too impossible to consider.

And then, at the bottom of the tallest stack of socks she found them.

Baby mice socks, with their tiny whiskers, rosy noses, soft white tummies, and giant gray ears with pink insides. *So cute.* Adorable even. Cuter even than Minnie Mouse with her big red shoes and polka dot bow. *These are like her babies,* Daisy thought, *Minnie Mouse and Mickey Mouse's little mouse babies.* Daisy could almost hear them squeaking.

"I want this pair, Mommy," she said, holding the snuggly baby mice socks up to her mother who stood a few feet away shaking her enormous handbag and listening for the sound of change.

"Really?" her mother said. "You want mice?"

"But you said any pair I wanted," Daisy said. She was going to hold her ground. "'No questions asked,' you said."

"All right, Pumpkin," her mother sighed. "You win. You want mice crawling up your ankles. You can have them. Just don't let them loose in the kitchen."

So, she got them. The perfect pink-nosed mousies. Mandy and Matilda, she would call them. They were sisters. Little sisters. Her little sisters, like the ones she wanted but never got. "Sorry, Buttercup," her mother had said when Daisy had begged her for a little sister after their neighbors brought home twin baby girls when her father was still alive. "We can't afford any more kiddos in this house."

No more kiddos. So, it was her fault she couldn't have a baby sister, much less two little sisters, like the big sister next door. Daisy held her mouse socks up and gave them each a kiss. She couldn't let disappointment creep back into her heart.

As soon as they got home, Daisy pulled off her sneakers and slipped into her snuggly mouse socks and danced around the kitchen while her mother unloaded the shopping bags. Jumbo boxes of oatmeal. Sacks of onions with their flaky skins peeling and crumbling onto the floor that Daisy liked to toss into the breeze from the back porch. More bags of beans and rice and different colored lentils that her mother poured into giant empty pickle jars and set on top of the cabinets. No sweet treats. No juice boxes. No boxes of anything with secret toys hidden inside.

Like always.

But Daisy didn't care. Today, she had Mandy and Matilda Mouse. They were mighty, her little mice. Mighty and mischievous, she decided, after her first week with them. Mischievous like the cartoon mice she watched on Saturday morning, with her feet propped up on pillows in front of the TV so Mandy and Matilda could see their cousin mice on TV. They were getting braver, Mandy and Matilda, Daisy realized, wrapping themselves around her ankles, nibbling at her toes, squeaking when she walked, though only she could hear them. They called to her in mouse-ese. Cute little squeals that sputtered and screeched like her mother's car early in the morning, only quieter.

"I need a new fan belt," Daisy's mother grumbled every morning, rain or shine, but every morning still came the squeals. Daisy wondered if the fan belt was lonely. *Is it crying?* Or maybe it was just embarrassed, living inside what her mother called "this rattle trap monstrosity that's all we can afford, Chipmunk."

Her mother had a lot of funny names for her, but Daisy didn't mind. "Chipmunk" was one of her favorites. "Doodle Noodle," was kinda cute too, but she really didn't like "Skinny Bean." It reminded her of all the beans they ate and how sometimes she really just wanted pizza.

Daisy's mother's car let out one more screech that afternoon as they backed out of the parking lot at Daisy's school. It was a shorter screech, more like a shout. Daisy suddenly worried that maybe the screech wasn't an embarrassed fan belt but instead was a giant mama mouse that lived inside her mother's car. *Oh no, maybe it was Mandy and Matilda's mother, come to take them home.* She couldn't let that happen. *They're my sisters now. But what about their mama mouse? Maybe my sister mice are missing their mama?* She would miss her mama even if her mother never let her get what she wanted. Except her mice socks that one time.

Daisy bent and tugged and tugged at her pant legs, trying to get them up above her socks. Her ankles felt like the mice were trying to crawl up her legs. Maybe they heard their mama calling. Daisy needed to make sure that Mandy and Matilda could hear the squeal inside Daisy's mother's car to know if it really was their mouse mama calling to them. She pulled her pant legs up to her knees.

"What is wrong with you, Mousey Mouse Girl?" her mother asked, glancing at Daisy in the back seat. "Are your mousitos tickling you again? You really need to let me wash those socks, Sweetie. How about we give them a bath and put them to bed when we get home? Even mouse socks need to rest."

Oh, maybe that's it. Maybe Mandy and Matilda weren't hearing their mama mouse call. Maybe they were just tired and needed to rest, like her mama was "just tired" whenever Daisy wanted another story and another and her mother would kiss her on the forehead and stroke her hair and say she was "just too tired" for another story.

Maybe her mouse sisters were just trying to crawl off the socks and into bed like her mama crawled into bed after tucking Daisy into bed for the umpteenth time. *Oh no.* Daisy had to help Mandy and Matilda rest the way her mama helped her rest. She pushed off her sneakers and pulled the mouse socks off. They were sort of stinky and stiff, and Daisy felt bad that she hadn't taken better care of her mouse sisters. She looked at her mama, waiting for her to scold her for not taking better care of Mandy and Matilda.

$

Scold her like Grandma had her mama. Said that her mama should have taken better care of Daisy's daddy before he died. That maybe he wouldn't have died if Daisy's mother had done a better job.

It was not something Daisy was supposed to have heard, she knew that, because her mama had shushed her grandma right away and told her to keep her voice down so that Daisy didn't hear, but Daisy had been listening next to the door in her bedroom even though she was supposed to be asleep.

"That's all the poor child needs, Edith," her mama had said to her grandma, and she'd sounded mad, which was not something Daisy's mother sounded like very often.

Daisy closed her eyes. The fan belt or the mama mouse or whatever it was had stopped squealing and it was quiet in her mama's car on their way home from Daisy's school. Daisy hugged her mouse socks close to her and wondered how she could apologize to Mandy and Matilda for not being a better big sister.

"I will not have Daisy thinking that her father died because her mother did not take good care of him," Daisy's mother had hissed at her grandma in a voice that was low and sharp. "You know I took care of him, very good care of him. For the past six months I have done nothing but take care of him. Why do you think we're so broke? But he died anyway, damnit. The cancer took our precious Reynold. He died and I and Daisy and you will never be the same without him," her mama had said and then she'd started to cry.

Daisy had put her hand over her mouth when she heard that. She didn't want her mama or her grandma to know that she was listening, that she was crying too.

Just remembering her mama crying made Daisy start to cry all over again. She'd never heard her mother cry before and now she couldn't forget it.

Daisy pushed her mouse socks over her eyes, one mouse sister for each eye. She didn't want her mama to see her crying there in the backseat of their rattle trap monstrosity with Mandy and Matilda getting wet and soggy and stinkier.

Maybe they're crying too. Maybe Mandy and Matilda were trying to tell her something. Maybe they needed to go home. *That's it.* She needed to let them go. Like her mama said they needed to let her daddy go.

"Mommy," she said and held up her two perfect mouse socks.

"Yes, Puddinghead," her mother said, looking in the rear-view mirror at Daisy in her booster seat holding up her two perfect mouse socks, one on each hand like puppets.

"I'm sorry, Mommy," she said. "I think I need to let my mouse socks go like Daddy."

And before her mama could say anything, before she could call her by another funny name or tease her for being a silly head or even fuss at her for wasting one whole dollar of her mama's money, Daisy rolled down the window, kissed her new little sisters each once upon the nose, and tossed her baby mouse socks out into the grass on the side of the road where the squealing mouse mama inside her mama's car could find them.

Flounder

"One dollar." Ben's grandfather held a worn dollar bill in front of his grandson. "I'll bet you this here dollar I can catch something before you do, buddy."

"A dollar'll get you a bag of finger mullet, Fred." Chester, the old man selling bait out of the shanty off the feeder road at the end of the island, grabbed the buck from Ben's grandfather and stuffed it in his pocket. He stroked the sparse white whiskers on his dark chin and pointed to the bait. "Strong scent, them mullet. Good for flounder, Fred, if that's what y'all are fishing for, and it outta be. Ain't nothing else biting today."

"Yessir, flounder," said the boy's grandfather, handing both fishing poles to his grandson Ben to hold. The old man patted the inside pockets of his slicker, greasy and torn though it was, and pulled out an old pipe and a crumpled pack of tobacco.

Ben's grandfather set to stuffing his pipe, his sun-browned hands trembling so that strings of tobacco fell on the ground, and he hissed at them as they fell. Ben watched silently. The old man saw the boy watching him. *Watch your tongue, Fred,* the old man said to himself. *Boy don't talk much, so don't be cursing none to show him how.*

⚓

"Take him fishing, Daddy," his daughter Colleen had asked. "Get him out of the stables for a while. Boy needs to be with people sometimes. Child can't live by horse alone."

"Not like his ma used to, huh?" The old man had smiled at her, but his daughter'd just poured him another cup of black coffee and set his breakfast dishes in the sink.

"Ben's not like me, Daddy," she said. "Or like you. World ain't beat the tender out of him yet. And don't you be the one to start, you hear me? Be kind to him. Please."

You was plenty tenderhearted too, the old man thought, *least with them damn horses.* And again, the fragments came back to him as he sat there in his daughter's make-shift kitchen in the little home she'd made on the Texas shoreline, these ragged bits of memory and valor mixed up with years he'd lost to the bottle. He thought of Colleen's mother, of the cancer that took her so young, and the pain and terror he'd felt holding their young daughter by the hand, watching the preacher sanctify his wife's newly dug grave.

⚓

Chester the bait man scooped up a ladleful of shiny silver slivers into a plastic bag of seawater and plopped it into the bucket. Ben's grandfather shook off his memories and looked at his grandson.

"They look like they're just babies." Ben peered at the bag of mullet.

"Look like fish to me, son." Ben's grandfather smiled a weary smile at the boy. "Swim like fish, and sure as hell stink like fish."

"Fish is fish, son," the bait man said, giving the boy a rough tussle on his shaggy hair. "And generally speaking, fish stink some."

Do they stink worse than the stench of old age? Ben's grandfather thought. *Of an old man that ain't saved his only child?* And again, his mouth twitched for want of whisky, but he shrugged it off with a grunt.

"You're on," Ben said, suddenly lively as the old man had rarely seen him. "First one catches something wins a dollar, Grandpa."

The old man grinned at the boy, who stood soft-eyed and gentle-voiced before him, holding the old fishing rod and tackle box the boy's mother had once used as a girl.

Ben's grandpa stuffed another pinch of tobacco into his pipe, leaned into the bait shed, lit a match, and sucked the flame down into the pipe. The tobacco burned red. He puffed out a few mouthfuls of smoke and coughed. The tobacco smelled thick and sharp like horse dung. The boy wrinkled his nose and turned away.

The old man lit another match and puffed again on his pipe and looked at the boy, small for his age with lonesome eyes like his mother's.

He thought again of his daughter, Ben's mother, and the fury in her gray-green eyes that sickening night months before the boy was born.

$

"Let me do this for you, Jelly Bean," he'd said to her then, his words slurring together. She'd come rushing up to the tumble-down stable hand shack they'd lived in on the horse ranch in North Texas, leading the boss's yearling. The animal had been beaten wildly, by the boss no doubt, who'd tried to break her too soon, and the old man had helped his daughter unsaddle the young horse, black as crude, and stayed with her as she brushed it down and treated the whip marks with salve and fed it oats and stroked its muzzle the way the boy Ben had done to the self-same horse that very morning before he'd come fishing with his grandpa.

"Somebody'll have to pay for taking this here horse," the old man had told his daughter so many years ago. "And it might as well be me, for all I ain't done for you, nor your mama before that. Was me that sunk us down to living here like field hands all these years shoveling horse shit for that bastard."

"I paid for it already, Daddy," she said, "even if that SOB denies it, which he will do like he denies everything else he's done to this family and this horse and half the county that nobody dares talk about," and it was then he saw the look of her, his beautiful daughter, her hair matted at the back of her head and her clothes twisted and crumpled.

"What do you mean, you done paid for it?" he asked her, the words coming thick and dull out of his mouth, heavy as they were with whisky and cigarettes that night, though in his heart he'd known what she had meant.

She punched the air and cursed the world.

"I mean, I already swapped him a trade, Daddy," she answered him. "To get him to stop beating this poor animal. He got what he wanted finally, so let's just leave it at that and let this horse be. The animal's had a hard time of it, Daddy. Anybody can see that. Just let it be. I'll be alright. I'll think of something to prove this horse is mine now."

Ben's grandfather looked at his daughter that terrible night, lean and defiant, even haughty as she'd been as a child, motherless for all the world to see, but he saw the defeat there, beneath the set of her jaw and the black iron sear of her words. The horse's owner would deny it all, they both knew that. The beating, the barter, the devil's bargain she had made. And the back country law would believe him, bossman that he was, as they always did.

I'll help her, as best I can, he told himself. And, sure enough when the bossman railed about his stolen horse, the old man marched himself into the sheriff's office looking bedraggled and swore a blue streak that he'd stolen a horse—a coal black filly he'd found wandering whupped and raw across the boss's land out off of the old farm road down by the railroad tracks.

And sure enough, he'd taken the poor horse, he said, saddle and all, and sold it to drifter passing through, though he was damned if he could remember who he was, slumped down drunk as he'd been and broke down as the horse must have been for the beating someone, maybe even the bossman, had laid upon her. And they believed him, these small-town lawmen, and let him do his time down in Huntsville Prison with all the other robbers and thieves just to be rid of him for a while.

His daughter swallowed her pride, thanked him, and moved away. She drove off in the darkness with the young horse in a rickety trailer, far off from the Texas panhandle where the horse was born. She set up her little riding stable on the southern tip of Galveston Island and made herself a quiet life, a simple living all alone.

The boy came along months later, sired, the old man figured, by his daughter's barter in the night, but they never spoke of it, his daughter and he. They kept their conversations at the prison—such as they'd been—on business, a new horse or saddle, or the pleasantries of life—Ben's first words, first steps, his two front teeth, the tuft of sandy hair that jutted up into a cowlick, and over time the boy grew to six years old, far from Huntsville, but sweet and kind and gentle, a quiet boy, unlike the cruelty from whence he'd come.

Standing outside the bait shack beside his grandson holding the bucket of finger mullet, the old man suddenly felt a rush of tenderness and fear for the boy, just a child who couldn't possibly know the ugliness of this world, its steady creep into even the lives of the good ones, like Ben's mother.

"Take him out past the jetty near the old road, Daddy," his daughter had asked earlier that morning as she set the breakfast plates onto the drying rack. "Folks say the flounder is biting good over yonder."

He'd said he would and smiled at her, and she'd stopped and brushed back a stray strand of near-gray hair and smiled back at her father. He grinned the grin of a prodigal man and went to find his grandson Ben that morning, alone as usual in the stables, stroking the velvety muzzle of his coal-black mare, flecked now with a few white hairs across its nose. A beautiful animal still, sleek, and strong for all its suffering. *The pride of his young boy's life,* the old man thought, *the one thing that sets him apart from every other fatherless boy cross the bayou.*

Ben's grandfather shuddered in the wet autumn air and turned and spoke to the boy. "You ready to catch us some flounder, son?" He nodded to Chester and stuffed his tobacco back into his pocket.

The boy and old man picked up their gear and walked down the stretch of hard wet sand past the jetty. It was a public beach, but at 8:00 am on a holiday morning in November they had the place pretty much to themselves.

The old man put his hand on his grandson's shoulder to steady himself, wobbly as he was without drink, and he felt the boy straighten his back and pull himself as tall as his six years would let him. He hadn't seen the boy much these past six years, some of it his own damn fault and some of it the jail time he'd done for the sake of the stolen horse and his daughter and the trouble she'd have been in if he hadn't. It wasn't his first turn at jail, and odds were, it wouldn't be his last.

The old man looked down at the ground. The boy's small feet lightened the gray sand beneath him slightly as he walked, a halo of paleness bursting out from each footprint, only to vanish in the salty wetness rushing back to fill the void. He looked down at his own feet, clumping along in his old boots, pressing the gray-green lightness like the boy's eyes into big, bleak circles around each step. He coughed and the boy's shoulder jerked slightly beneath his old man's hand.

"Flounder, here we come," said Ben quietly, slowing his pace to let the wobbly old man he barely knew catch his breath.

"Yessiree Bob." Fred sucked on his pipe again though it had long gone cold.

To the old man's surprise, the boy took hold of his fishing rod. "Your pipe's gone out, Grandpa," he said. "Lemme hold your stuff and you can light it again."

"Right you are, Ben." The old man turned his back to the waves, stuffing his pipe again and leaning toward the sand dunes. He held his hands over the match and lit his pipe. The wind hurled the smoke away from them and it vanished in the air like breath on a cold blue day.

Then he took the bucket from the boy and bent and opened the bag of finger mullet. His hand shook as he tried to thread his hook through the gills of one, and the fish struggled against him. Again, he felt the pull of liquor and he righted himself. He took a deep breath and tried again and this time he got the hook through the mullet's mouth, almost dead now with the hook sharp inside it. The old man tugged on the hook and tightened it up.

"Hold out your hook, son," he said to the boy, and he held Ben's hand tight in his as they took the hook and dug it through another mullet's gills and out its mouth. The old man's hands were cold and stiff.

"You know how to cast this thing?" he asked Ben.

"Seen it done," Ben said. "Don't go fishing much."

Then the old man crossed behind the boy and helped him swing his fishing rod back and forth a few times before letting loose the reel and watching the hook and sinker sail far out into the surf. Then he took up his own reel and cast out his bait beyond the waves.

They stood there, holding their fishing rods, looking out into the Gulf, the wind blowing their slickers flat against their chests and the cool salt breeze whipping through their hair. Out at the edge of the horizon they could see the dim shape of an oilrig and farther still beyond a tanker bellowed. The Port of Galveston lay north and west. Farther up to the north, Houston's ship channel beckoned, waiting for ships and cargo that came and went, loading and unloading freight cars piled high with sulfur, yellow as egg yolks, and cotton baled taut beneath their sheaves of burlap torn and tattered as migrants, bounty from a crueler time bound for or from the great wide world beyond.

Grandfather and grandson stood, breathing in the seaweed smell of it all. Their lines ebbed with the rhythm of the waves and above them the seagulls cawed as seagulls do.

"Yes sir," the old man said at last. "I could sure do with some barbecued flounder tonight."

The boy suddenly lurched as his fishing rod bent forward and he put one foot out and leaned back and groped for the reel.

"I caught something!" Ben hollered and he began to jump up and down, the taut fish line see-sawing the air. "I did it! I did it!" he shouted above the wind, breathless from excitement. His line pulled and yanked.

"Hold on, boy." Ben's grandfather stepped back and jammed his own pole into the looser sand behind them, angling it back so the line slacked then stretched taut again. Then he stepped up behind his grandson and put his arms around the boy. His hands over Ben's, they began in fast turns to reel the boy's catch in.

"Gonna get me a dollar," Ben muttered as the flounder flew out of the water and splashed back down as the old man and boy pulled it in. It flipped and flopped in the shallow sea brine, and the old man let go of the rod and grabbed the line and walked over to hold the fish up above the foam.

"Yep, looks like you done won that dollar, son," he shouted to the boy running up behind him.

But then the boy stopped. He reached out and touched the thin flounder as it struggled and grasped it between his hands, stroking it like a hurt pup flailing against fate.

"Let it go, Grandpa," the boy said quietly, his eyes suddenly fierce like his mother's. "Please, let it go."

And Ben's grandfather, his hands not shaking so much now for lack of drink, looked hard at the boy, the Gulf breeze slapping his hair across his face, and he saw the same sorrowful fury there he'd seen in his daughter that night more than six years before, and suddenly he felt the same sick helplessness sweep over him, busting his heart into a thousand splinters.

The old man gently pulled out the hook from the flounder's mouth, and the boy, holding the wiggling fish in both arms now, wadded into the surf and gently let it go.

"Don't need no dollar no how, Grandpa," he said. "'Leastwise, not that way, I don't."

Coughing again, the old man went and got the bucket of finger mullet and handed it to the boy.

"I reckon we don't need no dollar's worth of mullet neither, son," he said softly as the salt air stung his eyes. "Nosireee Bob, I reckon we surely don't." And as he watched, his grandson Ben, smiling now as he'd never seen him smile before, whooped and kneeled and let the silvery finger mullet dart out into the foamy undertow.

Boogie Board

One dollar! Jeez, the cool one was just a dollar more. Evan jerked his head around and looked out the window at the empty parking lot. *That's all, just a stupid dollar, but no, we can't spend one more stupid dollar to get the damn boogie board with the red flames on it. Stupid mom. Stupid money. Stupid boogie board. What kind of stupid dweeb rides a boogie board anyway? Stupid beach. Stupid fucking vacation. This is going to suck.*

Thunk. Evan slammed the door to the old Ford Fairlane. *What an ugly, dumb old car. Why don't we have a decent ride like regular people?*

Then he heard the screaming.

Jesus, what's that sound? He covered his ears as the desperate noise grew louder. It was like no sound he'd ever heard before. *What the hell is going on?* He swung his thirteen-year-old body, all legs and shoulder blades, around back to the car, back to the back door of the back seat where his knees had ached moments before as he'd tried to sleep, pretzeled between the dinged-up ice chest and the discounted flowered boogie boards his mom insisted were good enough for one round at the beach, nevermind how juvenile they made him look, like some kind of girly girl, and why couldn't he have a real surfboard anyway like the cool dudes really doing it, riding the waves, not just boogie boarding with their dumb old mom.

The howl grew louder and stranger and louder and stranger until it scared him.

He started to call out to his mom, but then he saw her there in front of him, with this horrible sound coming out of her. "Mom!" he shouted, scared now that this woman, his mom, was suddenly screaming bloody murder like some woman in a horror film. "Mom!" he cried louder.

"Get the key," she screamed, "In my bag! Unlock the door, Evan, unlock the fucking door!"

What the fuck? But then he saw it—his mom, who never stopped moving, never stopped taking care of business, was frozen to the side of the Ford Fairlane, the little finger on her left hand pinned in the door jamb of the car's back door he'd just slammed shut.

She was yelping "*nnn ... nnn ... nnn*" like a wounded dog.

He looked around. *Where's her bag, this thing that's like a part of her, like some black hump that grows on her side. Where?* Then he saw it, on the hood of the car, out of her reach.

With the quickness honed from hundreds of wipe-outs on his longboard, he lunged for the bag, dug into its bottomless unknown, and pulled out the keys with the wooden cheetah keychain he'd carved for her out of a branch at camp four years before. He found the car key, unlocked the driver's side door, and, in one motion, unlocked the back door and swung it open.

His mother slumped to the ground beside the car, whimpering, her body folded over her hand like the corner kids lighting their cigarettes on a windy day.

He slumped down beside her and put his arm around her and rocked her back and forth the way she had done, jeez, like a million times before.

"God, I'm sorry, Mom," he said. "I'm so sorry," and suddenly they were both crying, stupid laugh-crying, and rocking back and forth together there on the asphalt in the parking lot at the end of the beach while streaks of gray sand blew across it. "Here." He reached for her injured hand, limp and ashy and helpless as it was.

One by one he gently rubbed her other fingers, her ring finger that still wore her wedding ring even though his dad had been dead, what, five years now, and the middle finger he saw her raise only once when a road racer nearly ran them down on their way to his first baseball game, and the index finger and thumb that, well, were always busy chopping or folding or typing something.

"Coach Wells taught me this after I jammed my finger in practice once. You remember, it swelled up like a boiled hot dog you said. Thanks a lot, by the way," Evan said. "Took me a year before I could eat a hotdog again. Anyway, it confuses your nerve endings, Coach said. They're so busy sending massage messages from the other fingers that there's not enough juice left for the pain messages. Cool, huh?" Evan glanced over at his mom.

"Yeah, cool." His mom's voice was quiet and shaky.

"Is it working?"

"Uh huh," she nodded and closed her eyes.

"I'm sorry I bitched about the boogie board, Mom." He rubbed her ring finger with both his hands. "It's just a dumb boogie board; it doesn't matter. I just want you to be alright."

"Yeah, I'm sorry I was such a tightwad about the extra dollar, buddy." She opened her eyes. "All I ever really want in life is for you to be happy and for me not to worry anymore. That's worth so much more than a dumb dollar." She smiled weakly and bumped him gently with her shoulder.

"Yeah, I know." He pressed softly on each of her fingers. "I'm already happy, Mom. I just want your pain to stop."

His mother laughed and ruffled his scraggly bedhead with her other hand. "That's the sweetest thing a boy can ever say to his mama. You keep working on that until you're thirty-five, OK?"

"OK," he laughed and rubbed his mama's fingers as the seagulls wafted in the breeze.

Evening in Paris

One dollar in her pocket, Willa Rae looked all about. She'd never been inside the store before. Had never dared breach the jingling glass door her ma had told her not to enter. "Our kind ain't welcome there, baby. Best leave it alone and move on by," she'd told Willa Rae when they first got to these parts for the picking season. "Don't need no trouble now, you hear, Willa Rae? We got trouble enough for the whole wide world and all the worlds beyond."

Willa Rae had promised, she'd sworn to her mama that she'd be a good girl like she asked, but then she'd found the dollar, old and tattered and fluttering along the side of the road like a magic butterfly, and Willa Rae'd made up her mind to see the store for herself.

A wonderland it was too. Spools of red and purple ribbon, buckets of bright blue plastic petunias. Rows of rick rack, racks of spice. Buttons and bouillon and socks. Willa Rae's head spun, and she grabbed ahold of the glass counter to steady herself.

She closed her eyes and breathed through her mouth the way she did at the camp latrine.

She tilted her head back and opened her eyes and there, up near the ceiling on the tip top shelf, she saw it, that deep blue bottle with fancy writing. She'd seen it before, in catalogs in outhouses, on signs in shop windows, and once, in the panhandle of Texas, she'd peered into a window with lacey white curtains beside the road and there it had been again, this blue, blue bottle with a shiny silver top like a bullet sitting on a dresser top doily.

And now here it was again, the very same.

From out of nowhere, a dime store lady with a powdery pink face and silver blue hair appeared and started wiping the countertops though they were already shiny clean. She looked at Willa Rae with a hungry meanness that made Willa Rae think of the old woman trying to eat the gingerbread man in the story her mama used to tell them, but Willa Rae didn't care. She kept her eyes on the blue, blue bottle up high on the shelf.

"Please, ma'am," she asked. "How much is that one there?" She stretched her chapped, sunburnt hand up toward the big blue bottle. The lady looked where Willa Rae was pointing and clucked a deep, gurgly lady cluck and turned back to Willa Rae.

"Oh honey, that one there's a whole $2.00. You got that kinda money, child?" The lady's baby blue eyelids blinked as she glanced at Willa Rae's frayed gingham dress stretched tight across her tiny budding breasts.

"Oh, yes ma'am," Willa Rae said.

The dime store lady coughed a phlegmy cough, but Willa Rae didn't pay it any mind.

"You sure about that, girlie? It's a mighty hard trial to get it down and a body's got to be careful these days, what with all the riff raff coming through." The lady smiled stiffly. The powder cracked at the corners of her mouth.

"Yes ma'am, I surely do," said Willa Rae and, clutching the dollar bill behind her, she doubled it over and flashed it before the lady quickity quick.

The lady grunted and bent down behind the counter and grabbed a metal claw device sitting beside a rusty fan. She held it in both her hands and stretched her soft, round lady arms up and up to grab the blue, blue bottle of *Evening in Paris* cologne, eased it off the shelf, and set it down before the girl.

Willa Rae opened it and sniffed.

It smelled like sweet, sweet womanhood, sweeter than sweet, and Willa Rae closed her eyes and thought of her ma and her hard, red hands smelling of Pine Sol and smoke and lard. She thought of lace curtains and doilies and pink and blue posies blooming in ladies' gardens in the villages they'd passed through these past five years going field to field of oranges and carrots and cotton. She thought of all the doilies on all the dressers in all the ladies' happy houses across the land, and then she thought of her ma bent over a creek bed scrubbing dirt from dungarees.

"Smells nice, don't it, girlie?" The lady smiled a closed-lip, prissy kind of smile that made the rosy circles on her cheeks dimple.

"Oh yes, yes, ma'am. It surely, surely does." Willa Rae smiled, and as the lady leaned to set the claw down, Willa Rae, her hands trembling, her scraped knees bent and ready, slapped her dollar bill down on the counter, grabbed the blue, blue bottle, swung open the jiggling door, and ran and ran and ran as fast as the Gingerbread Man.

Airport Caddy

"One dollar? Just to rent a stupid cart?" Gillian lets her hard suitcase plop to the floor.

Airport caddy, the sign says. *To lighten your load. Put the pleasure back in traveling.*

Christ, why the hell did I bring this dinosaur suitcase along? What was I thinking? Gillian sighs. Is she trying to re-create some bourgeois traveling experience of her childhood when her mother had insisted that her girls wear dark wash-and-wear dresses, thin plain white socks, and black patent shoes, straps down for Marilyn the oldest, straps up for Gillian the younger?

Back then, she remembers, they'd used Sky Caps, those hard-working human caddies in red hats who could glide a dally full of luggage through a crowded airport like an Olympic skier slaloming down the Alps. "Thank you so much, young man," their mother would have said to the dark-skinned man who would have smiled that surface smile that always fooled rich white folks, Gillian's mother notwithstanding, as she sailed through the airport like Grace Kelly herself, fluttering

101

her white-gloved fingers at the check-in gate. Tipping his red hat, the man would have nodded his head ever so slightly as Gillian's mother pressed the crisp dollar bill into his discreetly unfurled palm, and off he'd go, his dally racing behind him as the three of them—"Girls of the World," she'd called them in her best Rosalind Russell voice—stepped up to the ticket counter.

Back then each little girl had carried her own pint-sized "makeup kit," as if six- and seven-year-old girls needed makeup, carefully packed with child-sized Oral-B soft toothbrushes and Pepsodent Tooth Powder, tiny soap bars from some Holiday Inn their father had stayed at, and little shakers of Johnson's Baby Powder to prevent blisters. Gillian and Marilyn had wrapped their Tinkerbell shampoo and crème rinse in pink washrags and stuffed them inside plastic sandwich bags, just in case, their mother cautioned, the glass bottles shattered in the altitude.

Back then, Gillian remembers, cargo holds weren't pressurized.

Back then, I wasn't pressurized, either. Back then, time stood still, at least for their mother, who moved through the world like the Sky Caps did, sliding past all obstacles in her path, a smile on her face, and dollars in her sensible black pocketbook.

God, how did she do that? Gillian pulls her overfilled handbag up on top of her suitcase and begins the search for an elusive dollar. There, at the bottom of her bag, she finds one, crunched up next to a ballpoint pen leaking sticky blue ink all over the face of George Washington, all over the white lining of the thrift store purse, all over Gillian's ungloved hands.

"Great. Just great," she says, wiping off the shiny midnight blue smudged across three fingertips and a knuckle. "This would have never happened to my mother," she mutters, remembering her mother's hands holding theirs as they boarded the plane where the smiling beauties then called stewardesses handed them each a box of Chiclets to chew as the turbo prop plane rumbled down the runway and lifted up into the air like a water ballerina with wings.

Back then, their mother would have straightened her skirt beneath the seat belt, lit up a Viceroy cigarette, and settled back for a well-deserved smoke.

Back then, Gillian wouldn't have noticed any of it—not the Sky Caps nor the white gloves nor the ease with which her mother dispensed dollars—but now, ten hours into her transcontinental sojourn, she really, really wanted that airport caddy.

So Gillian, whom her mother had called her dear, sweet, nonfrivolous girl, Gillian the miser, Gillian the tightwad, Gillian, the only solvent member of her family now, rubbed the shiny blue ink off the face of George Washington with the underside of her hem, smoothed the worn dollar bill into the slot, and, with a silent prayer to the patron saint of discolored faces, pressed the lever forward and magically, the airport caddy rolled forward, bumping Gillian on the toe and offering itself up to her, the bone-weary traveler, with the same earnest brawn the pallbearers would show tomorrow at her mother's funeral.

"Oh darling," Gillian knew her mother would have said seeing her daughter lug the suitcase onto the airport caddy, "Not everything needs to be so hard. You deserve a little respite once in a while. And sometimes all it costs is a dollar.

"Just one little dollar, dear."

The Gutter

One dollar.

One whole silver dollar.

Her life savings.

Gone.

Fallen out of her pocket into the gutter below.

The girl tried to look into the opening, but her head was too big and the darkness down there scared her.

Daddy says there's rats down there. Don't go sticking your hands down into that gunk, baby girl. You need a dollar, your daddy will give you a dollar. New and shiny as that diamond ring your mama's always talking about. Don't you never go getting yourself into some dark hole just for a lousy dollar, precious. Not for one dollar, not for ten, not for all the dollars in the world, you hear me now, baby doll? You listen to your papa now and keep your hands outta the gutter and sparkling clean.

"Dear dollar," the girl whispered into the depth. "Remember me. PS: Be careful, dollar, my daddy says it's dangerous down there."

The Gutter

One dollar.
One whole silver dollar.
Her life savings.
Gone.

Ice-Cold Water

"One dollar! Ice-cold water, right here."

A young black man wove between the cars hovering at the intersection of North Capitol Street and New York Avenue in the nation's capital.

Jack watched the sweat roll down the man's dark face and drip onto the faded emblem of his 'Skins football jersey. The man pulled a gray cloth from his back pocket and wiped his face.

"Ice-cold water," the man shouted to the shiny Nissan Maximas humming around him, their AC's revving the cars' engines to a brutal groan.

The red light lingered.

Jack watched his father watching the water man many cars in front of them. His dad's ruddy midwestern face had turned bright red in the humid swelter of DC. His dad had never been to Washington before, not that Jack knew about anyway. He didn't much care for cities, Jack's dad didn't, and certainly not this part of this city.

"Get your cool drink of water right here. One dollar!" the water man sang to the tinted windows. Here and there an opaque mirror of glass silently rolled down enough for a dollar bill to appear and an icy bottle of water to disappear inside.

Jack glanced at the sidewalk next to them. Old men lounged outside the corner liquor store smoking butts. Three young women walked by, dragging toddlers by the wrists. One of them fretted about the cost of Pampers.

Jack draped his arm along the open window of his '71 Corolla and watched the water man move toward them. He felt his father tense and glanced over to see him rolling up the window on the passenger's side, neverminding the oppressive heat.

Jack sighed. He thought of his dad's tirades against the urban poor on the East Coast. "Lazy sons of guns," he'd call them, watching the news reports about crime in the cities. "Damn scofflaws. Parasites living off the likes of you and me, buddy. You and me and your mother there, lying in a cold, early grave. Your mother worked herself to death, she did. Double shifts from the dawn of time. People don't work the way she did, son. Not anymore. Not them hooligans. You stay away from them damn crooks, buddy boy, bleed you dry."

Jack hadn't, though. Stayed away. Instead, he'd moved here, to the nation's capital at the height of the crack wars. Beirut, people called it on the news. Beirut on the Potomac. Murder Capital of America. Drug-Lord-in-Chief Rayful Edmond III was in charge, Marion Barry was Mayor for Life, the War on Drugs was raging, and the body count kept rising.

Pop, pop, pop, went the night.

$

Jack's father had begged him not to go after his mother died. To leave the home of his birth, of his mother's grave, his sisters' children, and his dad's empty, rickety house. But Jack, with his Nebraska Cornhuskers t-shirt tucked into his Levi's, had hopped on to the expressway and driven across the Great Plains of America to be a third grade teacher in Southeast DC, aka America's largest open-air shooting gallery. *To help salvage the children,* he thought, *from Nancy Reagan's Land of Just Say No.*

His father had not understood.

"Why you gotta go off and live in that cesspool kid, with all them lowlifes? Ain't life good enough for you here? And what about your Scout Troop? Who's gonna look after them when you're gone? Those kids love you, Jackie boy. They'd do anything for you. Life don't get any better than that," his father had said, but he'd looked at Jack with the same ground-down despair Jack had seen flicker in his own eyes after Caroline, Jack's girlfriend, had left. Suddenly married a Marine she'd met at the USO and moved to Camp Lejeune, North Carolina.

"I know, Pop," Jack had said, trying to shake off his loneliness lest he become his father. "And maybe you're right. Maybe it doesn't get any better than this. But I have to find out. I have to see if I can do this. Get out of Nebraska and make ..."

Jack had stopped himself from saying it—*make something of himself*—words he knew he could never take back. Words he'd spent his whole life avoiding.

Even then, his father's face had already begun to fall at the mere suggestion of those words, seeming more and more at the ready every day for this harshest of truths. That life in Nebraska was invisible to the big wide world and Jack wanted to be seen. Unlike his dad whom nobody saw at all anymore.

Jack's dad had taken on a resignation so deep it was irretrievable. And it had begun to suck up Jack as well in those days. After Jack's mother died and Caroline left. This abyss no longer visible to the naked eye.

"Make some kind of a *difference*, Pop," Jack had said instead, looking his father in the eye. "Some kind of real difference. Out in the world. I'll be back, Pop. I will. Every holiday, every chance I get. I promise."

His father had swallowed and looked away, out to the ridge of prairie grass that met the sky, the auburn sun shimmering in the day's demise.

"Just don't become a slacker, son," his dad had said.

Jack had struggled not to cry.

"Show me a man can do an honest day's work, and I'll show you what this country is made of." Jack's father had tightened his jaw and twisted his head to one side the way he did. "Them raggedy-looking gutter bums back east ain't worth the twitch of a dead chicken."

"Pop, you can't say crude things like that these days," Jack had told him over and over again. "People won't put up with that kinda talk anymore, and you'll get your old fool self fired and then where will you be?" And he nearly had, Jack's dad, gotten himself fired for cussing out a black guy at the ammo plant for clocking out early one day a few months before the plant closed down for good, and Jack's dad and the black guy and damn near every other working stiff in the county had lost their jobs and all that remained for them was Al's Bar and Grill and the small respite found in the brotherhood of drinking men.

"Ice-cold water, folks, one dollar," the man in the sweat-soaked 'Skins jersey bellowed again, raising his bottles of cold water high in the mid-day sun and letting the condensation from them drip down his bare arms.

The red light turned. A dozen cars crept through before the light turned again.

Jack inched his Corolla closer to the intersection and waited for the next go round.

"Ice-cold water!" The water man pulled four cold new bottles out of his cooler covered in burgundy and gold stickers of the Hogs, the beloved offensive line of DC's football team.

The ice-water man was moving toward them now. Jack watched him approach and looked over at his dad.

"Who is this guy?" his father asked. "Is he here all the time?"

"Every day, Pop," Jack said quietly. *Please*, he silently prayed, *don't let Pop make a scene.*

"And that's all he does, sell water? He don't try to sell you no drugs or nothing?" his father asked.

"No, Pop, just cold water."

"It always this hot here?" His father wiped his forehead with the sleeve of his shirt.

"Always, Pop," Jack watched the light, waiting for it to change. "DC's built on a swamp, people tell me. Come August you can tell."

"Well, that's the damn truth," Jack's dad said.

"Water! Ice-cold water for the working folks!" the water man sang, getting closer.

From a couple cars ahead of them a woman's tawny arm stretched out holding a dollar, and the man handed her a water.

Jack flipped on the fan from his broken AC, but it only blew out air that was hotter than the outside, so he clicked off.

"He out here every day?" his dad asked.

"Every day, Pop, rain or shine." Jack gripped the gear shift tighter.

Jack's dad suddenly rolled down his window. Jack tensed and jiggled the gear shift in neutral.

Jack's dad grunted.

Yep." Jack pushed in the clutch and gave the Corolla a tiny bit of gas. The car rolled forward slightly. *Turn green already. Come on.*

"He by himself?" Jack's dad looked around. Suddenly, he shifted his weight and reached behind him.

"Pop!" Jack sputtered, stomping on the brake pedal.

"What?" his father said, pulling his wallet out of his back pocket. "What the hell did you think I was doing? Gonna shoot the guy or something?"

Jack laughed. He took a deep breath and thought of the pistol his father had bought when Jack was born, and how he'd promised Jack's mother that he'd never let anything happen to them.

Jack lightened the pressure on the brake pedal. He watched the light. *Still red.*

"You thirsty, son?" His father pulled two dollars out of his wallet.

"Parched," Jack said, and suddenly he was.

His father reached over and patted Jack's shoulder.

"Hey, fella," Jack's dad shouted to the water man.

The ice-water man looked over at them.

"Two ice-cold waters, please," Jack's dad said.

The water man trotted over, shaking the condensation off the outside of the bottles.

"Here you go, mister. Ice-cold water for the working men." The water man handed the waters to Jack's dad and shoved the two dollars into his pocket.

"You betcha." Jack's dad nodded his head ever so slightly at the water man. The ice-water man wiped his brow with his arm and nodded ever so slightly back. He stepped toward the car behind them.

"Wait, son," Jack's dad said suddenly, and the water man turned.

Jack stared at his father.

Jack's dad pulled another dollar bill out of his wallet.

"Drink one for yourself, young fella." Jack's dad handed the man the dollar. "It's hotter than Hades out there and a working man's gotta stay safe. You stay safe now, hear?"

Jack started to speak, but just then the light turned green, so he shifted the car into first, eased up on the clutch, and gave the old Toyota a smooth pedal of gas the way his dad had taught him years ago.

As they made their way slowly through the intersection Jack's dad twisted his body around, stuck his right arm out the window, and waved to the water man, who took a long swig of water and waved back.

"Water, ice-cold water, one dollar!" the water man shouted to the newly stopped cars as Jack and his dad disappeared down the road.

Brothers and Sisters

Starry Lashes

One dollar's worth of stamps spread across the front of the envelope like a portrait gallery of early American icons.

Hope's sister Claire was like that, always scattering random bits of history into everyday life. History was something of a hobby for Claire, had been since they were girls sneaking into their father's study late at night and poring over the war books there.

Smiling, Hope opened the envelope and pulled out a gray folded piece of cardboard with the word *Remember!* scrawled in Claire's flamboyant hand.

Inside was a single snapshot, a grainy black and white picture Hope instantly recognized from their mother's photo album. They were at the beach, the girls sitting in the shallow water letting the sea foam around them. Claire had plopped a clump of seaweed on Hope's head, and they'd screamed with laughter just as their mother had snapped the shot.

In the photo, Hope's wet eyelashes clumped together into starry points that gave her face a harlequin look.

Daughter of jest, she thought. *Lear's Fool in the making.* She held the photo in her hand, remembering the frothy saltiness that had elated them as children, the days at the beach, the sea-bulb bonnets she and Claire used to make—ugly droopy things filled with plankton and marine life they couldn't see or even imagine.

Perched with the seaweed on her head, Hope looked sweet and lightly pretty, the way children do. She looked again at the picture and there it was—the elasticity of a child's skin, clear and rosy even in black and white.

A remarkable quality, Hope thought, *this childness, unaware of itself though so obvious to others.* The species perfected, unabashed and unashamed, the child wearing her childness in the roundedness of her cheeks, in her look of pure delight, in the starry clusters of her sea-wet lashes.

Something from behind the picture, some warm, invisible hand seemed just then to reach out and touch the flat bone of her chest as if to massage her weary heart beneath, pumping away moment after moment a whole life long. The revelation passed through Hope like a soft coastal breeze over the damp, summer skin of childhood.

She felt a moment of pure aliveness plucked from moments of lesser joy. *These—these pristine moments—are the whole of your life,* she thought, *for the rest of the body.* And she thought of those bits of greater joy captured and recorded on the surface of things—on pieces of photographic paper, certificates of birth, cool plaster poured into a pie tin and pressed against the ridges of a baby's fingers, pressed as these moments are pressed into the wetness of memory.

The picture of herself as a child had this effect on Hope, and she wondered why her sister had sent it to her, what had possessed Claire to send her this small piece of herself. She felt a sudden and deep sadness, mourning life itself, ticking away into the past as it was, evaporating into ever more distant memories shared by fewer and fewer people.

Oh God, she thought, *don't let Mama die.*

And then Hope was lost to it, lost to the tears that came when she envisioned her mother, poised and proper still, lying in serene surrender upon her pillow, her thinning hair spread out gently around her head as Hope brushed it. She'd speak softly to her mother then of trifling things, moments they had shared, a peach cobbler, a burst of music, a look they'd both remembered in the eye of a stranger on some bygone street. It was a pilgrimage for Hope, going to her mother's side, and she found a solace there she found nowhere else.

And suddenly it was there again, that solace, wrapping itself around her as their mother had a thousand times. Hope looked down again at the grainy photo sent to her by her one and only sister. The whole of her life tucked inside a dollar's worth of postage stamps. And that, she realized, is what Claire must have thought of when she sent it to her sister.

The Tuesday Theory

One dollar. Ballard looked at his brother across the booth. Willis sat, arms pressed against his sides like always, staring at the lone dollar bill between them.

"Go on, take it, Willis." Ballard gently pushed the dollar toward his little brother. "It's your turn, bro, to give Miz Eileen the tip," he said, his voice soft like their mother's had been. "It's Tuesday, remember? Tuesday's your day, buddy. Share a dollar on Tuesday, and nothing bad can happen. That's our theory, remember? The theory's everything, buddy."

"Has the theory ever been wrong, Ballard?" Willis asked, not lifting his eyes and looking at his brother like a brother would.

"Nope, the theory's never been wrong, Willis," Ballard answered, and in that moment he believed it, this crazy theory he'd suddenly invented, there at the diner that first Tuesday morning after the funeral when he and Willis, each in the grip of a grief that had no words, had tried to have breakfast without her.

Their waitress Eileen, her aging eyes even softer and kinder than they usually were, had come over to their regular booth, order pad in hand when Willis, poor Willis, had swept the condiments and salt shakers and tip money off the countertop and crawled under the booth, beneath the underside rippled with gum wads and dried ketchup and who knows what other kinds of diner crud.

Eileen had held Manny the cook and other waitresses at bay while Ballard crawled under there with Willis, sat down on crunched sugar packets, and scooped up a lost dollar bill, and that's when it had come to him. *The Tuesday Theory*. He'd held out the dollar bill to his brother like it was a dog biscuit and Willis was the golden retriever they used to have, before it died too. "Share a dollar on Tuesday and nothing bad can happen," he'd sworn to his little brother. Over and over and over again until Willis and Ballard and even Eileen, God Bless her, who'd crouched down under the tabletop with them on her arthritic knees, had vowed together. They'd nodded their heads, solemn as undertakers, and sworn an oath that nothing bad would ever happen on Tuesday so long as they followed The Tuesday Theory.

And now three years later, sitting there in the same booth in the same diner, the same grandmotherly wait-ress Eileen bringing them their food, Ballard, for a second, believed again as he wanted Willis to believe with his whole heart. In the theory, the scientific maxim that their lives were moving with the invisible force their mother had believed in, moving inextricably forward toward the light, as she called it, toward the center of the universe that was the three of them when she was alive and they were a family united, together forever. Like she used to say when Ballard would wake in the dark, frightened, and there she would be, her soft hand on his young boy's forehead hushing him with certainties lest he wake his little brother sleeping there across the room.

Ballard cleared his throat and looked at his brother, who'd grown taller than him over time, taller and thinner. Ballard watched Willis peer at the dollar bill laying Washington-side up on the top of the diner's table. A few stray grains of salt radiated out around it like distant moons. The thick white dishes that had held their over-easy eggs and hash browns and toast and Ballard's coffee sat neatly in the stack Willis had made, breakfast plates on the bottom, then the saucer and the jelly bowl nestling the lone coffee cup like a fat hen on top. Willis had stacked the silverware together—two forks, two spoons, two knives—and tucked them into the space between the dinner plate and saucer so they wouldn't jiggle.

Ballard had placed the dollar bill in the middle of the table the way he always did on Tuesday mornings.

"Has the theory ever been wrong, Ballard?" Willis asked again, still with his arms tight against his sides.

Ballard brushed the salt off the table into his palm and sprinkled it into the coffee cup. "No, Willis," he answered. "The theory's never been wrong, OK?"

Willis leaned and placed his palm above the dollar bill, letting it hover an inch away. He made a slow circle clockwise over it, clicking his tongue in rhythms like radar.

Ballard watched this rotating ritual of his brother's. Willis's way of working the theory, this ritual inside a ritual. It used to bother him, this clicking-tongue, hand-revolving habit of Willis's, especially when he'd done it at school in the lunchroom or the library or anywhere where the regular kids were. The other kids, of course, especially Dennis O'Malley, had been merciless and cackled and pointed and called Willis weird and scrawny and a dumb crazy jerk, and Ballard had punched O'Malley in the mouth and gotten them both suspended from school for a week.

"Yeah, crazy like a fox," their mother had whispered to Ballard and hugged him as they'd sat in the principal's office defending his defense of his brother.

"Crazy like a fox," Ballard said suddenly aloud. "Eh bro?" he muttered and glanced across the diner, looking for Eileen.

Willis didn't answer. He still hunched over the dollar bill, his ear nearly touching the table, his hand still moving clockwise, his tongue still clicking.

Ballard sighed and the green Formica of the tabletop suddenly felt cold under his elbows.

Maybe our mother was wrong, he thought and then shook his head and cleared his throat as he tried again to push that thought away, though back it came. They hadn't been united forever, hurling ever forward toward some beautiful reward. She had died, and maybe that was her reward, maybe that's all there was anyway, just one day after another of making the best of a bad lot. Then everlasting darkness and cold and painless sleep. *Maybe that's all there is,* he thought. *Maybe nothing else will ever change. At least not for Willis, no matter how hard we try. So then what?*

Ballard watched his brother clicking his hand over the dollar bill in the same ritual, unchanged as it was for the past many years, since Willis had been eight years old and Ballard was in middle school. Their mother was still alive then, and Ballard, well, he was still just a happy kid gobbling perfect pancakes on a Sunday morning.

"Find any defects yet, Willis?" their mother would ask her youngest child as he hovered his hand over her perfect flapjacks, clicking away like a Geiger counter. "No defects yet, huh, buddy?" she'd asked again, and Willis would shake his head and keep revolving his hand over and over his pancakes until at last their mother would bring the syrup over.

Sputtering like a Red Baron bomber plane from the First World War, she'd shout "Duck and cover, Willis. Here comes the syrup bomb!" And Willis would grab his head with both hands and duck under the table, howling like a siren. Their mother would rain Vermont's finest over Willis's ten perfect pancakes and Willis would screech that rare screech of delight he has.

Ballard misses those screeches of delight. Oh god, how he misses them.

Ballard looked around the diner again. It was early still and most of the regulars had yet to arrive. At the side window a couple of cops sat drinking coffee. Ballard recognized the older officer from when he used to patrol the high school, what five, six years ago? Officer Palacios, or something like that. His hair was still combed back in a fierce shock of salt and pepper, more salt now than pepper but formidable all the same.

The younger cop stared at them. Ballard sighed and gave the cop a tiny smile, nothing sinister, just friendly and harmless like he had shown Willis how to do. The young cop, though, nudged Palacios and pointed to Willis hunched over the dollar bill, rotating his hand and clicking.

Ballard tensed, his tiny smile vanished, but Palacios shook his head and waved his hand in the air, dismissing his partner's concern. He glanced at Ballard and nodded his head slightly.

The barest of greetings.

Ballard relaxed and leaned down to catch Willis's eye the way their mom used to, the way Ballard had come to do never knowing, though, if it would work for him the way it had for her.

"Hey buddy," he said. "Remember the theory? Share a dollar on Tuesday and nothing bad can happen? It's time to share that dollar."

"Has the theory ever been wrong, Ballard?" Willis asked.

"No, buddy, the theory's never been wrong," Ballard answered. "You ready to share that dollar now, Willis?"

"But Ballard, has the theory ever been wrong?" Willis raised his eyes for one quick glance at his brother.

"No Willis, I promise," Ballard said quickly, startled by his brother's glance. "The theory's never been wrong. You ready now, bro?" His voice rose with excitement. "I know that Miz Eileen's gonna be real happy when you give her that dollar tip."

"Has the theory ever been wrong, Ballard?" Willis repeated, his eyes diverted again.

"Never wrong, Willis. Never wrong," Ballard whispered, and he caught Eileen's eye and she winked at him, tucking a strand of white hair behind her ear and pulling her order pad out of her pocket.

"Hey Willis," she said as she got to their booth. "My Lord, is it Tuesday already, hon?"

Willis stared at the dollar bill. "Share a dollar on Tuesday, and nothing bad can happen," he said.

Willis turned toward Eileen, his eyes still fixed on the dollar. "Has the theory ever been wrong?" he asked.

"Not once, buddy," she said, her eyes crinkled and patient like their mother's had been as she waited for Willis's eyes to meet hers. "Not once in all the years you've been coming here on Tuesdays, Willis." She tilted her head down slightly as she always did.

She glanced at Ballard and smiled a small hopeful smile that seemed to say Maybe the theory will work this time, son. Maybe Willis will look me in the eye at last. Maybe Willis will be okay after all.

"The theory's never been wrong." Willis clutched the dollar bill. "The theory's never been wrong. The theory's never been wrong." He raised his eyes high enough to see the waistband of Eileen's apron, then he held out the dollar bill, his arm straight, his elbow rigid.

And Eileen, grasping the dollar bill between her thumb and forefinger, gently pulled the bill from between Willis's grasp.

"Thanks Willis," she said softly. "You have made my Tuesday again, buddy. The theory's going strong."

"The theory's never been wrong," Willis whispered, and slowly, as Ballard and Eileen watched, barely breathing, Willis raised his eyes and met Eileen's and gave her that tiny, harmless little smile his brother Ballard had taught him to.

Gas Station

"One dollar, please," their mother said to the scrawny white boy who came out to pump their gas. She handed him a crisp new bill and he looked at it like he'd never seen a new dollar bill before.

"Do you have a ladies' room?" their mother asked.

"Don't work," said the boy.

"Oh." Their mother smoothed the collar of her cotton dress. "What's that?" She pointed to an outhouse set back from the road. The wood on the wobbly structure had silvered and grown smooth and shiny in the East Texas heat.

"That's for the coloreds," the boy said. "You don't wanna use that."

Their mother pursed her lips and looked the boy dead in the eye. He stuffed the dollar bill into his pocket and walked over to the pump.

"Wait here, girls." Their mother opened the car door.

The boy stopped pumping their gas and stared at their mother.

Maddie and Gwen watched her walk her straight-backed walk over to the dilapidated structure. The hinges had rusted on the door with the word "COLORED" scrawled in red paint, and it creaked as she opened it. A multitude of flies swarmed out as Hannah Macmillan disappeared inside. The door bounced gently behind her.

Maddie and Gwen glanced at the skinny boy and gripped each other's hands. The stench from inside the outhouse had wafted over to them, and they wrinkled their noses. Across the way, a floppy-eared old dog barked on its chain. Maddie and Gwen prayed for their mother to get back soon.

Suddenly, a big woman in a pink striped dress came out of the gas station and walked towards them. Her short cotton sleeves stretched across her upper arms like cellophane around a loaf of bread. The boy finished pumping their gas and handed the dollar bill to the woman.

Must be his mother, Gwen and Maddie thought, and they looked back to see their mother approaching. Neither Gwen nor Maddie could read yet, but they knew their ABC s and what words were. They knew that those red letters on the outhouse meant it was for colored people, not blue-eyed white ladies like their mother.

"You got some kinda problem, lady?" the big woman asked their mother as she got back into the car. "Something couldn't wait for the next fillin' station down the road?"

"She looks mad," Gwen whispered to Maddie.

"Yeah, mad as that old dog over there." Maddie pointed to the animal that had stepped up its barking as soon as the woman spoke to their mother.

"I most certainly do have a problem," Mrs. Macmillan replied. "It's a barbaric practice, these 'COLORED' toilets; you should be ashamed of yourself, madam, participating in this travesty."

"Well, that's just the way we do things 'round here, *miss*," the woman said. "You don't like it, go back to where you come from."

"Mama," Maddie whispered to her mother. "I gotta go."

"Men's bathroom's working," the boy said to their mother, pointing over to the white door with black words painted on it. She could use that."

Don't go in there, Madeline," the girls' mother said. Maddie squirmed in the back seat. "That's a wicked, wicked place that bathroom there. I don't want to ever see either of you pass through a door with those words on it."

As the big woman watched, Mrs. Macmillan spelled out each letter on the white bathroom door and made Maddie, the older, say them with her out loud. "'W-H-I-T-E-S-space-O-N-L-Y.' Whites only, girls, that's what that says. If you need to use the restroom, children, and the bathroom ever has these letters on it, you will either hold it or you will use the one with those letters over there," and she pointed to the red letters on the outhouse off to the side away from the dog. "I don't care what kind of fuss people make about it, girls—how much they tell you to use the better bathroom–it's wrong to use any toilet that's got those ten letters on the door. There are ten letters there, girls, and until such time as you can both read, I want you to count the letters."

"All right, Mama," the girls said in unison, and suddenly the big lady leaned over and peered into the back car window. Her bosom pressed against the side of the car, straining the weave of her dress.

Maddie and Gwen sat very still, not breathing, watching the lady, not saying anything as their mama had told them children were expected to behave out here in Texas pine country.

The woman's body blocked out their view of the woods as she raised a roughened red hand and held it just over their heads, like a faith healer blessing the little children.

Maddie and Gwen felt something like static electricity fly between the tuffs of their thin blonde hair and the woman's hand. Their mother, they noticed, had turned around. She sat very still watching this woman examine them, Hannah Macmillan's jewels, people called them, in their newly washed shorts and clean-cut fingernails.

"My, but these girls," the big woman said, "are like two perfect pecan halves split open without a crumble between them."

"Yes," their mama said softly. "Yes. they are."

"Yor mama's some kinda stubborn lady now, ain't she, sugar bits?" the woman said to Maddie and Gwen, not looking at their mother who sat straight and still in the driver's seat.

"Oh, yes ma'am," Maddie concentrated on stretching out the words the way their daddy did.

"Yes ma'am." Gwen added. "Stubborn as a rat-bit mule, Daddy always says."

And with that the woman exploded in a thunder of laughter that swept the girls up in it like a mudslide on a treeless hill. Gwen and Maddie, relieved and bewildered, held onto each other as they laughed lest they wet their pants and their mama fuss at them for ruining their new summer outfits.

The woman opened her mouth wide, and the girls could see the teeth inside her squishy pink mouth that reminded them both of jolly old Saint Nick. And it was only July.

Then the woman stopped laughing. She took the crisp dollar bill out of her pocket, crumpled it up, and threw it at the girls.

"Go on, now git," she snarled. "Git yer rat-bit old mama outta here. Y'all don't come back now, hear. We don't want your kind comin' 'round here, you hear me?"

And with that, Hannah Macmillan, her back so straight it didn't even touch the seat, turned on the car and drove her girls away.

The Forgiveness Man

"One dollar for your troubles!" In the corner of the Dollar Store parking lot, just outside the faded yellow line beyond which no shopping cart could roll, an old man in flapping dungarees stood shouting atop a milk crate.

One by one people hurried past, clasping the pudgy hands of their toddlers tighter, wrapping the straps of their handbags over their chests, scanning the strip mall for familiar faces. It was early evening on a summer's payday, and Californians came and went, their bags filled with detergent and diapers and sheets.

"Lay that baby buck down over here," the old man roared, "and I will give you a gold mine of forgiveness, an abundance of absolution."

A young woman with a newborn bundled in a ragged green snuggly stopped and stood gaping at the man. The breeze blew his sparse gray hair back and a mangled red ear appeared. The young woman's baby stirred, and she hushed her with a dainty hand.

A heavyset man in dark blue coveralls ambled over, the emblem of his employer smudged with grease. He studied the old man's face. A treasure map of scars it was, leading to some long-forgotten bounty perhaps. Perhaps not. Who's to say? The man's wife joined him, shielding her eyes from the setting sun and deepening the furrows of her face.

"See, this here forgiveness is my gift," the old man said softly, looking straight at the young mother transfixed before him. "I carry on these two boney shoulders all the sins of all the people," he said, "'cause folks done did to me damn near every wrong a body can do to another—beat downs, slap arounds, whippings. Humiliations. Thievery, lies, betrayals. Carnal knowledge, covetations, callous disregard. Treachery, treason, equivocations."

The heavyset man glanced at his wife, the remnants of contrition etched across his face.

"You name it," the old man continued, taking in the small crowd gathering before him. A pair of scruffy skateboarders slouched at the edge, their sun-blond hair falling over their beach boy eyes.

"Any violation that leaves a body bloody but still standing, that there's been done to me," he said.

"So, I figure," the old man shifted his gaze back to the young mother in the front, "I got the right to forgive anybody anything. That there's my gift. And I will share it with you good people."

A sob broke out from the young mother and her slumbering baby flinched, her tiny limbs jerking inside the snuggly.

"Whatever it is, sweetheart," he stepped off his crate and bent toward the young woman weeping before him, "whatever sins of the fathers or the fathers' fathers you been carrying around with you all these years, one hug from these arms will bring you a feast of forgiveness."

The young woman took out her last dollar and gave it to the man, and he wrapped his spindly arms around her and sure enough, she felt a peace come over her that she'd been without so long she thought it stillborn inside her.

Just then her baby woke and the piercing, staccato *ah-ah-ah* of a newborn rose. The old man laid his rough hand on the child's tiny head, and she quieted.

Folks looked at each other, their doubts assuaged, and a line formed in front of the old man.

$

And so it went, up and down the California coast that summer of my first year of life. She traveled with him from June through August, my mother said, leaving behind the ragtag band of other runaways she was living with in an abandoned gas station.

She let go of abandonment itself that very evening—she told me years later when I was grown—and decided then and there to keep her baby no matter the cost, and she threw the whole of her young, wounded heart into spreading the old man's redemption with him. Down they went, this peculiar pair with an old milk crate, into the crevices of canyons filled with migrants and the recesses of communes and campgrounds filled with the newly evicted.

The Forgiveness Man, they came to call him, my mother and all her fellow Forgivens, the bedraggled godless who'd left their grandmothers' religion behind, the heathen and damaged, and those dying with their sins uncleansed.

Word spread and the people came.

Thieves came emptying pockets of stolen objects.

Bosses came heavy with wages denied.

Errant lovers came for reborn fidelity.

Addicts came bent with remorse.

Fathers came yearning for families lost to idleness.

Mothers came grieving for children spurned by second fathers.

All manner of humanity flowed to The Forgiveness Man.

They laid their dollars down and The Forgiveness Man stepped off his crate and wrapped his burned and battered arms around them, young and old, dark and light, the stooped and the upright, the sober and the strung out, humbled folk from all the discarded chapters of lives undone there in the Golden State.

So went the stories that my mother told and told again in the last year of her good life, fervent tales that had become the fables of our family.

And favorite among them was the story she told often at the end, of how she and our father had finally found each other again there among the forgiven folks that summer, and how the old man had blessed them—this young couple with a tiny babe—and how he'd held them close, and sent them out into the world with the gift of the first dollar my mother had given to him that day in the parking lot, and all the other dollars the people had given to them in their few months together.

Dollars, the old man said, the girl—and her baby—had earned learning how to forgive.

And so, as she lay dying my mother gathered our family around. She unfolded the Forgiveness Dollar, she called it, this weathered old bill that had bought her absolution so long ago from the Forgiveness Man.

Over the years she had placed it in our hands many times, my brothers' and mine, whenever we'd been troubled or fearful or ashamed, and our mother had stood before us, and we had handed her the dollar, and she had wrapped her thin arms around us and conjured up her Forgiveness Man, to keep us whole and safe and bound to each other.

And now, once again we stood before her, and one by one passed the Forgiveness Dollar from us to her, and she hugged each of us close, and we felt the sweet release of forgiveness pulse through us one final time, one damaged sinner to another, and we let the salty wetness run down our faces and fall onto the ground.

Known Associates

Exact Change Only

"One dollar? Shit, there's a friggin' toll? On the 'Po White Parkway'? Stupid Richmond. *Virginia.* Still sticking it to the poor whites, I see. That's me, you know, ain't I a "po white?" God, a toll! When did that happen?"

"Jerry? Wake up!" He shakes the zonked-out passenger.

"I swear to God, there never used to be a toll. Mother of God, fucking highway robbery. So much for cops and robbers, man. Friggin' cops are robbers now, man. Yeah, I'd like to see them do five years hard time. Five years, two months, seven days, twelve hours, and eighteen minutes to be exact. First-degree burglary, my ass, nobody was supposed to be home. Yeah, you fuckin' swore to that, didn't you *Jerry!*"

He pokes the sleeping Jerry.

"Jerry the Pirate. Jerry the Pea-Head is more like it, and you getting goddamn probation. *Probation!* Shit, whole thing was your idea."

He shakes Jerry again.

"Hey, wake up and gimme a dollar! Christ, you're out like a light. Fucking 'ludes, man—you been asleep the last five years!"

"Shit, roll over so I can check your pocket, asshole. Jesus, when did you start 'buckling up,' fool?"

He tries to move his friend but he's too heavy.

The car in front of him rolls through the toll gate. He inches forward.

"Crap. Exact change only. After 11 p.m."

"How the hell's a guy supposed to have exact fucking change? You know how long it's been since I had any change, sucker? Five years, two months, seven days, twelve hours, and eighteen minutes—no, no, nineteen minutes—to be exact. Waiting in this goddamn lane. Shit. Got me a twenty and that's it."

"Jerry, wake the hell up, I need a dollar." He shakes Jerry harder. Jerry doesn't rouse.

"Fuck. Forget it."

The car behind him honks.

"OK, OK, lay off the horn, asshole!" He glares in the rear-view mirror at the car behind him.

"Oh god. Exact fucking change only. I've only got a twenty, you stupid robot. The hell I'm gonna give you my life savings." He rolls up to the toll bucket.

"Oh, and what's this? 'Turn off my wipers, *please*?' Oh yeah, you gonna make me you little blink, blink red light? Huh? You wanna take my picture?"

He turns his wipers on high.

"How's that, swish, swish, swish. Here, have some squirter juice, you dumb fuck. Squirt, squirt, squirt." He sprays the windshield with wiper fluid. "Goddamnit Jerry—wake the fuck up!" He screams at his friend.

The driver behind him blasts his horn.

"Stop honking! All right. I got to think. Crap. One dollar exact fucking change."

The car honks again.

"All right, all right! Fucking toll." He leans his head on the steering wheel.

Behind him, the car honks again, longer.

"Quit your damn honking, jackass! Shit, here goes, buckle up. Oh well."

He shifts the car into gear.

"One dollar, my ass."

He floors it and breaks through the wooden arm at the toll gate.

"Crash! Take that, you little blink, blink red-light motherfucker!"

He shoots the finger at the toll gate behind him as he races away.

"Woo-hoo!" He laughs. "Hot damn!"

Dolores

"One dollar." Dr. Peter Lanford held the crisp new bill in his hand and waved it in front of his dinner companions at the awards banquet honoring him and a few other aging members of the Texas Medical History League.

They were dining at the renowned Elderton Club, where—legend had it—back in the sixties, the British matinee idol Sir Reginald Wellington used to light ladies' cigarettes with $100 bills and beguile them with stories of saving damsels in distress on the silver screen. After which he'd lure the lady smokers up to his suite for a meaningless tryst.

Peter had seen him do it, once, as a fifteen-year-old bussing tables on the night shift. Peter'd been only a table away and the movie star—though he wasn't a star anymore then, just a broken-down has-been wasting money on sallow young women—had regaled a debutante-to-be with another tired old tale of derring-do and laid the flaming hundred-dollar trick on her when the girl's doctor dad came back from an emergency phone call and belted the old fart in the kisser. The actor's toupée had flown off his head and landed in the décolletage of one of Houston's most revered doyennes.

Dr. Lanford, ever the extrovert, had told that story many times, in this very club no less, to these very colleagues, before he'd been bitten by the humanitarian bug at the dawn of the new millennium and gone off to the wilds of Patagonia or some such place to save lives.

Or so the story went.

"Here we go again," Dr. Frank Tremaine said from his table near the stage, dipping a jumbo boiled shrimp into the horseradish sauce and stuffing it whole into his mouth.

"Enough is enough, Peter. Let the old geezer rest in peace," whispered Dr. Rachel Schumacher from her fellow-honoree chair onstage. She was the youngest of the award winners but by far the most conciliatory. It had been her older sister, after all, whom the now-long-dead matinee idol had propositioned some forty years before.

"One dollar," Dr. Lanford repeated, his voice rising, his palm hitting the lectern with a decided *splat*. The rest of his colleagues looked up, their cocktails tinkling to sudden stillness.

"Is something wrong, Peter?" Dr. Cynthia Ward asked discretely from her Mistress of Ceremonies chair. They had dated in med school, but she'd gone on to marry a fellow dermatologist with regular hours, unlike Peter the bachelor who even then was leaning toward epidemiology and the wide world abroad.

"One dollar," Lanford repeated, his voice hushed this time, his lean, tanned frame bending toward the dollar fluttering before this room full of distinguished physicians. "One dollar a day, ladies and gentlemen of medicine, that's what your colleagues in global crisis zones can spend per patient, per day. Maximum."

A mutter of vague annoyance rippled across the room, low enough to be anonymous, loud enough not to ignore.

"One dollar." Dr. Lanford focused his icy blue eyes on the table nearest him where the major donors for the History League's Memorial Donation Program sat.

"That includes all medicine, all nursing care, all bandages, IVs, saline, plasma, you name it. As for MRIs, CAT scans?—Forget it!" Lanford snorted. "X-rays, maybe, God willing, if the generator's working, you might get one, maybe two films a day, circa -1950 quality. One dollar, my dear colleagues. That won't even buy the mocha in your cafè latte here in Houston. One dollar. *Un dolar.* Change the inflection, amigos, and you have *dolor.*"

Lanford paused.

"*Dolor,*" he said slowly, "the Spanish word for pain. *Dolor,* meaning sorrow. *Dolor,* meaning anguish. *Dolores.*" He let the "es" sound linger. "The plural, meaning many sorrows. Dolores, as in she who suffers."

He stopped and looked out at the crowd.

"Let me tell you a story, friends, about what this one dollar could do for a little girl named Dolores."

Dr. Lanford clicked on the slide projector and a giant image of a small Mayan girl appeared, strands of dark, matted hair laced across her face. Her eyes were heavy with infection, her meager countenance witness to the tiny lives lamented in world hunger ads on Sunday morning TV.

"Dolores." Lanford leaned into the microphone, his starched collar digging into his chin. "Her very name means suffering. Suffering in a way you and I and your children and your children's children will never know, have never known."

"I met her when she was only six years old. '*Mi nombre es Dolores*,'" she said to me when I first met her, and she hung her head. '*Pero todo el mundo me llama la pequeña abandonada, la desgraciada.*' My name is Dolores, but everyone calls me the little abandoned one, the disgraced one.

"Abandoned by a mother too sick and poor and beaten down to care for her, Dolores lived at the garbage dump, *el basurero*, of her rural community, among the street urchins that were the lowest of the low on the descending ladder of poverty. In *el infierno de los condenados*—the inferno of the damned. When we found her, she was curled up on a ragged mattress, eating rotted mangos, her eyes covered in flies.

"She had acute trachoma, granular conjunctivitis that left only a sliver for her to look out of. Her skin was ashen and covered in open sores. She weighed a mere twenty-five pounds and was half the height of an American child her age.

"Malnutrition, infection, dehydration, trachoma, diarrhea. Take your pick of pathogens and pathologies, they were all there living inside of tiny Dolores, she who suffers. But not anymore. Not anymore."

Lanford turned to the projected image behind him.

"This"—he shook the dollar bill again, violently, like a dying can of spray paint — "this tiny dollar changed all of that. We brought Dolores to our field hospital and for ten days we pumped her full of electrolyte fluids and antibiotics that this dollar paid for."

Lanford grabbed his wallet and pulled out another dollar bill. "For ten days we fed her a bland diet that cost *less* than a dollar a day. We bathed her crusted eyes with saline antibiotics that this dollar paid for."

He pulled out another dollar.

"And on the tenth day, when she was bright-eyed and smiling, we gave her a new doll—her very own baby doll—that this dollar, the same meaningless dollar that you all spend every morning for that caramel *macchiato,* paid for."

Lanford clicked and a new slide appeared behind him of a sweet and smiling girl, her eyes bright, her long hair woven into a gleaming braid, her clothes fresh and clean. She looked up at the camera hugging a baby doll wrapped in a striped blanket.

"And for the first time in her young life, Dolores, *la pequeña abandonada,* was whole and healthy and happy. While we sit here in this lavish hall drinking our pisco sours and sucking down shrimp as big as a Texas long-horn, this dollar is saving lives, saving families, saving nations, saving the world. It's a miracle."

Peter Lanford stopped and stared at the audience.

"Miracles, my friends, isn't that what we all dreamt about when we were kids who wanted to grow up to be doctors, way back in those moments before we fell asleep, our six, eight, twelve-year-old heads sinking into the soft pillows on the warm beds we grew up with? Doing good. Helping people. Wiping out diseases. We dreamt about that, you and you and you." He pointed to the well-groomed physicians sipping their cocktails before him. "You and I dreamt about that—though we'd never admit it in medical school, of all places, not on the ward, not in the OR, and sure as hell not in the Emergency Room where the broke and bedraggled go in this great land of ours.

"No, good works cease to exist once you enter the cynical world of the medical establishment, but some-where—deep down between the ninth and tenth hole on the golf course, perhaps, in the split second on your skiff before you trim the sail, or as your debutant daughters in their thousand-dollar gowns sweep down the marble steps of your country club, your childhood dream of working miracles reappears, and we remember.

"So, remember now, colleagues. Miracles do happen. They are just inches away, inside the calfskin of your wallet, the silk lining of your Gucci bag. Roll out those platinum American Express cards. Open your hearts. One dollar, ladies and gentlemen, for Dolores.

"One dollar to believe again. Best deal in town."

On the screen behind him the logo of the global health organization appeared, with a website and 1-800 number followed by an entreaty to "GIVE NOW" in bright, bold letters.

Here and there a doctor's wife gasped, startled by Dr. Lanford's blatant fundraising.

"One dollar, Doctors. The power is all yours. Thank you."

Lanford looked out over the banquet room where his fellow physicians greeted his final remarks with polite applause. Whispers about broken protocol wafted about the room. A handful of young volunteers began weaving through the crowd, encouraging donations.

Dr. Lanford took a final swig of the Evian water before him and stepped away from the podium and off the stage.

"Christ," he muttered, "I need a cigarette." He grabbed a tall-neck Corona from a passing waiter and headed to the emergency exit in back.

The hot, humid air in the alley outside hit him like a shot of Haldol. He felt heavy and dull, and he closed his eyes and slumped against the brick wall. *Why am I still trying to get these asshole doctors to actually give a shit?*

"That thing you said, about the dollar..." It was a woman's voice; it startled him.

A dark-haired woman, forty, maybe forty-five, stood a few feet away, her arms crossed over her crisp white employee blouse, her cigarette poised before her. A slight woman with the barest of smile lines, she stood quite still, slowly flicking the thumb and little finger of the hand holding her cigarette.

"Oh." Lanford reached into his jacket pocket for his hidden cigarettes—the last of the smokers among the physician class. "You heard that, did you?"

"Yeah, I was working the bar in the back." She dropped her cigarette to the pavement and snuffed it out with her toe. The cuff on her pressed black trousers swayed once, then fell back into place.

"Well, this crowd must have kept you damn busy."

"Ha! That's true. You doctors can really put it away."

Lanford tipped his Corona to her. "Salud," he said. "Thanks for keeping us lubricated."

"So that business with the dollar," she straightened her pressed blouse, "is it true?"

"You mean can a dollar really buy all that? Yeah, it can. Not that those fuckers really give a shit. Not anymore. They just want to be seen looking all humanitarian."

He took out one of the dollars he'd stuffed in his pocket.

"This little baby can change a life." He waved it weakly in the dank alley air.

The woman reached out and slowly slid the dollar bill out of his hand.

"So where can I send my dollar?" She twirled the dollar bill around her bare ring finger and fluttered it before her like a diamond ring.

"Really?" he asked.

"Yeah, really."

"Let me give you my card." He reached into his inside pocket and handed the woman one of his business cards. "That's my private number at the bottom," he said.

"Oh," she said. "*Gracias mil.* Good to know."

"Another?" Dr. Lanford tapped two cigarettes out of his pack and offered the woman another smoke.

"Sure, what the hell." She took the two cigarettes, offering one back to the doctor. "You?" she asked.

"Of course," he smiled.

He pulled out the steel lighter that had gone with him from field hospital to field hospital and flipped it open.

The woman leaned forward, her left hand cupped over both cigarettes between her lips, the folded dollar bill jutting out on her right hand.

Dr. Lanford suddenly plucked the bill from between her fingers, lit one end of it with the lighter, flicked the lighter closed, and leaned forward to light the two cigarettes in the woman's lips with the burning dollar bill.

The woman laughed a light, lilting laugh that defied the swelter around them. She brushed back the graying hairs on the side of Dr. Peter Lanford's face.

"So, do you wear a toupée also?" She leaned and drew deeply on the flame and the tips of both cigarettes glowed red and ashen.

"Oh, you've heard that story too, have you?" He let the burning dollar flutter to the damp concrete pavement.

"Everyone's heard that story," she said. "Doctor Lanford."

"So, you know my name," he said as the woman handed him his smoke. He took a deep drag and exhaled high into the night air. "But I don't know yours."

"Oh," she smiled, tapping the ash off her cigarette. "It's Dolores."

Dr. Lanford paused. *"¡Ah, por supuesto!"* He smiled. *"¿Estás abandonada, Dolores?"*

"No, I'm not abandoned, but," the woman lifted her chin up and blew three perfect smoke rings toward him, "I could use some shelter from the storm."

Dr. Lanford grabbed at the smoke rings, but they vanished in the air. "I can do that."

"Yes, I thought you could. Peter," she said, and she flung down both their cigarettes and ground them out with the tip of her black leather flats.

Boiling the Buggers

$1.00. I need to hold a dollar. In my hand. Across my palm. To calm me down. I need to calm down.

A headline scrolled across her laptop screen. The virus was spreading. China, Italy, New York, the whole USA. Novel corona virus disease 2019. CO-VI-D-19. Death and dying spreading exponentially.

"Oh God." She closed her eyes to the fragments of memory. Biology class. Microscopes. Petri dishes slathered with microorganisms. Gentian violet-stained bright purple bacteria that the teacher swore were harmless. But she knew. Even then she always knew that was a lie.

Deep breaths.

She opened her eyes. A new email flashed open, and she bent to read it even as she felt it closing in on her.

"Shit," she said. There it was, the clarion call of her life collapsing. She clicked off the email with the news of her layoff. Of everyone's layoff. She pressed her palms to her forehead. She was all alone.

She slammed her laptop closed. She needed to regain control.

Go get a dollar from the cookie jar.

She looked toward the kitchen. A fat ceramic jar covered in purple flowers sat on the counter. Next to it was an antique napkin holder filled with white cocktail napkins stamped with the logo of the bar she worked at. All unemployed now. Indefinitely.

The sick feeling hollowing out her belly deepened. She needed this job. The paycheck, the tips, this apartment she had finally found for herself right before her mother died and now there was nowhere else to go.

"Damn. Damn. Damn," she muttered. *Everything was going so well,* she thought. *You were finally normal. Christ. Laid off. You can't be laid off. Not now.*

She wrapped her arms across her chest. She had to stop this.

Get that dollar, girl. Hold it in your hand. Let it work its secret OCD magic.

She went into the kitchen and reached for the cookie jar where she stashed her tips every night in ritual celebration of her triumph over her germaphobia.

Suddenly she stopped, her hand in midair, pallid and clammy. She stared at her palms.

"Oh God, no," she cried. It was starting again.

Her hands, it seemed, were crawling with the virus. Thousands of predatory pathogens writhing and wriggling across her palms, her fingers, her wrists. Germs. Germs. Crawling everywhere. Just like they used to do before all the therapy. All the meds. All the delay, delay, delay the OCD rituals like the therapist said. "Change the ritual. Change the response." All the role playing and practicing and pretending to be David slaying her own Goliath.

She shook her hands.

"Get off!" she sputtered, and wiped at her hands, at the invisible vermin contaminating her again.

She turned on the faucet with the back of her wrist the way she used to and with her elbow pumped hand soap *one, two, three*—always three—and began to wash and wash and wash her hands. The germaphobe's first ritual of purification.

"Out, out, you parasites!" she snarled. She ran her hands under the faucet and imagined the microbes sliding away, slithering helplessly down the drain,

Gone.

"Cleanse your hands, you sinner," a preacher on her Granny's Sunday church show had said and she had remembered it.

She opened the bottom drawer with her foot and took out a clean cup towel.

Do not come back, you bloody germaphobia. Do not do this, she thought.

She dried her hands, three long, slow strokes from her wrists to her fingers, the sanctity she found in threes.

She pursed her lips and breathed out slowly.

You beat it, remember, she told herself. *No more germaphobia. Do not let it come back. You worked too hard. You*

got a job. You made money. You have a life. An independent life. You showed them all.

It had taken her ten years to overcome this. Ten years of peering inward, staring down her obsession with germs, smothering it into submission. Ten years of white knuckling through therapy slowing her down, breaking the patterns, inching her closer and closer each year to touching that doorknob, grabbing that bus strap. Ten years of first this drug, then that. Ten years of talk, talk, talk before she could finally stop washing and washing and washing her hands after every meeting or meal or minor encounter with the billions of unwashed surfaces on the planet.

Ten years searching for forgiveness, for baptism, purgation, peace.

"Fire and ice, Lord," her granny used to say and then she would quote scripture, "We shall pass through the fire, and be clean, child. Wash us, and we shall be whiter than snow."

Fire and ice, she had thought as a child. *They must be magic.*

"Fire and ice," she said.

But she had done it, one microbe at a time. Exposure therapy they called it.

"First, pet a dog," said her therapist.

Then: "Dig a garden."

Stick your fingers into the dirt and feel those microorganisms all around you.

She had done that.

"Now, get a job," said the therapist.

Something unsanitary. Something dirty.

And she had done that. Gotten a job. And not just any old job, with its run-of-the-mill germs.

She got a job awash in microbes.

Bartending. Mixology. She had immersed herself in the sweat and filth and grime of nightlife and become a barkeep, tending to dirty, drunken souls. Ceremonially sprinkling water into their drinks, sparkling tonic. Restorative and pure.

She'd thrown herself into her new livelihood with the same OCD precision she had brought to her quest for purification. Salvation through mixology—concocting with an alchemist's passion for combining mystical elements into curative brews. So many ounces of this spirit or that, a splash of Angostura bitters, a dash of salt, a wedge of lime, the list went on.

The Dirty Martini had become her specialty, an inside joke she shared with herself, clean freak turned master of the Dirty Martini. It was a dance, really, that she performed every night with her regulars. Her Dirty Martini devotees, Don and Dewayne and Deborah, who would come in from a day of pushing papers and order a round of Dirty Martinis, and she would get to work.

She would warm up her fingers—*one, two, three*—and gather the ingredients while her regulars watched—she the sanctifying barkeep and they her devoted parishioners. The Church of the Dirty Martini, they called it, and Deborah would laugh, and Dewayne would call dibs on the toast, and Don would watch her as she moved silently behind the bar.

She reached up to the call shelf behind her and took down the Stoli (if Don were paying) or Grey Goose (if Dewayne) or Square One, the favored domestic, (if Deborah was up), though when they were broke, they motioned silently for the rail brand, and she always complied. No money. No judgment. How could she? She just reached under the bar for the Smirnoff or Georgi and grabbed the vermouth, the Martini & Rossi, the extra dry, unless of course it was payday and they asked for the primo. Carpano Bianco. *Italiano speciale.*

Out came the Spanish queen olives or manzanillas, off came the screw tops, and the jars sat waiting on the counter for the barkeep to pick up her shaker, the polished, monogrammed steel bullet of her trade she had bought herself when she'd landed the bartending job.

Get a job. Something dirty.

She held the shaker, cold and smooth and painless, and filled it three-quarters full with crushed ice.

She held out her two-ounce jigger like a test tube in chem class so long ago, and measured, slowly, six ounces of vodka—*one jigger, two jiggers, three jiggers, done*—and poured the clear hard liquid into the shaker. Next came three splashes of vermouth and three of brine, a glance, a shy smile at Don who sat following the dance of her hands as they shook and shook the shaker. "Just shake it, don't stir," she murmured to Don, like James Bond to a priestess. A full thirty seconds of silent movement, just her and the shaker and Don holding his breath, until the Dirty Martinis were colder than cold.

She set down the shaker gently, gently like a crystal vase, and reached into the freezer behind her to pull out three chilled martini glasses and slowly, carefully strained the martinis into them, the brine curling slowly like a rip tide. She speared two olives each and perched them, pimento-side up, on the rim of the glasses. Cleansing the bar for the tenth time with her bright white towel, she laid fresh cocktail napkins down and softly set the Dirty Martinis in front of Don and Dwayne and Deborah, an offering to the Martini Gods. They lifted their drinks between their fingers like communion wafers and brought them to their lips in unison.

Rebirth by libation.

"Oh darlin'," Dewayne exhaled. "You know how to rock my world." And Deborah, not to be outdone, reached over and squeezed his thigh.

Sometimes Don, when he was feeling especially flirty, would order a round of "Filthy" Martinis with a wink and curl of his lip—which had thrown her at first (*A man? Could I really be with a man? Another human being? What is that like?*) but she had just grinned and added two more dashes of olive brine. Then, looking at Don like a gangster's surgeon extracting a bullet, she'd pulled out the pimento with a toothpick and waved it before him with a smirk. (*Where did you learn to do that, you flirt? Do you know what you're doing?*) Grinning, she'd gulped down the pimento and wedged in a sliver of bleu cheese in its place.

"Now that is a dirty, filthy martini, my lady," Don had said, looking truly debauched, and she'd smiled a triumphant smile.

Damn, girl, you have an exquisitely normal life, she had thought. *Bravo.*

Every now and then a weathered old guy—Gus, she thought was his name—would amble in and order a Jameson's neat—*neat*—and she and he would share a smile, one *neat* freak to another. She took special care, measuring an ounce and half of the amber liquid (adding another half pour as a reward)—a prize for the man who takes his liquor neat.

Neat to neat.

And then, then would come the real payoff—after the Dirty Martinis and the Jameson's neat and everything in between—came the sliding of dollars across the bar—three ten-spots from Don for the Filthy Martinis, two fivers from Gus, peace offerings to her OCD heart. She took the bills and held them beneath the bar and ran her fingers once over the face of Washington or Lincoln or Alexander Hamilton, then again once across the bill's back, and finally once across the Treasury seal in a long, slow swipe, the magnetic pull of money soothing her, calming her fluttering heart with her *one stroke, two strokes, three strokes. Divine,* she thought, *like Granny.*

It had saved her, this secret ritual she had made for herself. Over and over she would do this all night, three long strokes of the bills in the same direction, no one ever the wiser, and then she'd open the cash drawer and lay each bill to rest in its own special bed with its brother and sister bills. The ones here, the fives there, tens next door, twenties off to the side. The rare fifty or hundred slipped underneath.

Oh, it had been glorious, these secret nightly delights across her palm—delight after delight all around really, her boss, her customers, the pregnant register growing fatter each night with the fruits of her labor.

But now she stood in her kitchen holding the towel and staring at the cookie jar. Inside were her darlings, her tips, her partners in fighting her obsession. Dollar bills, fives, tens, the occasional twenty.

Get your dollar, girl. Just hold it in your hand. Pretend like it's your pay. Your reward.

Her new ritual. The sweet balm of dollars crossing her palm, her balm in Gilead, her final ticket out of her phobia, out of the paralyzing fear of germs that had ruined her life for ten years. She had been a recluse living in her childhood room in her mother's house.

Unemployable. A freak.

Mocked by the very family she labored to protect.

She could almost hear her mother's voice coming out of the photo by the window in the kitchen.

She whirled around to the bookshelf filled with family photos, the few who had loved her, neverminding her affliction, and the ones who had clucked at her, blessing her heart with all the phoniness they had in them.

"Don't look at me like that." She pointed to the photo of her mom dressed in her signature sundress and straw hat with the yellow rose blossoms. "Don't you dare say it. Don't you dare tell me you told me so. That I wouldn't be able to ever be on my own unless I got over my—what did you call it? My 'irrational fear of germs. Little dirt never hurt anybody,' you said. *Oh God, Mama, how many times did you say that?*"

She stared at the photo of her late mother smiling coquettishly at the photographer. Next to it sat a photo of an old woman in a violet needlepoint vest, smiling a Mona Lisa smile. Her grandmother.

"But I showed them, Granny," she said. "I got better. I licked it. Germaphobia gone."

I petted that dog, she thought. *I dug that garden. I became a bartender, for Christ's sake, one step up from a garbage collector. A barkeep, surrounded by horny, drunk people pumping out who knows what kinds of secretions.*

"I mixed their drinks," she said to her grandmother's photo. "Their Dirty Martinis. Perfectly. I am a perfect mixologist, Granny. You would be proud of me. 'A genius with a shot glass,' Dewayne calls me. 'An artist behind the bar,' Don says. And I touched their money, their ones and fives and those dollars made me whole."

I lived a normal life.

She swatted at the air.

Until now, you microbial buggers, she thought. *Playing with the germaphobe. Is this some kind of sadistic joke?*

"I will beat you again, germaphobia. I already traded you in, remember? Swapped you for something that made sense, let me into the exclusive club called 'the mainstream economy.'"

Getting paid, she thought. *Having dollars cross my palm like an offering to the Gods. People passing me money from their hand to mine, their hand to mine, their hand to mine.*

She stroked her palm.

It felt so fine, she thought. *Holding that money. Making a living, earning my keep, bringing home the bacon—the trichinosis-filled bacon—on my own.*

"You stupid phobia," she muttered. "Don't you dare think you can just come back and muck this up."

Make me forget about my new secret one-two-three, hold-a-dollar, make me-normal ritual? she thought. *A nice, discrete sweet thing that nobody notices, nobody laughs at; it's just me and my fine, fine feeling holding that money. You think I'm gonna let you take this happiness from me?*

"And don't you start up with your damn 'I told you so's' like Mama," she hissed. "I don't want to hear it."

She was breathing hard.

"OK, calm down, girl." She wrapped her arms around herself again.

Let's do this thing, Stroke that dollar like it was money made. Non-essential worker be damned. You are essential.

She should wash her hands, she thought. Again.

She turned the water back on with her wrist, pressed down on the hand soap, and began to rub over and under her fingers, across her knuckles, above her wrists the way they she did for all those years, the way morning show hosts now demonstrate.

"Sing Happy Birthday twice when you're washing your hands," the perky TV hosts chirp, rubbing their manicured hands together and smiling at the camera.

Happy Birthday, hell, better to go with Lady Macbeth's soliloquy, she thought, remembering how it had spoken to her so long ago in high school English class, her teacher breaking the lines down into chunks of guilt and madness. *Guilt and madness, my old friends,* she'd thought, and secretly she'd begun to recite this speech of purgation as she washed and washed and washed her hands all those years ago. Over and over she had spoken it in her head, swaying back and forth over the sink, her eyes closed, the Bard whispering in her ear: "You are not alone." And from among the depths, he had beckoned a whole carnival of obsessed souls for her to rest among. Princes and queens, faeries and beasts, ghosts and betrayers, etched out in her mind's eye offering solace from her torments. They too knew the constancy of fears.

Now, standing in her kitchen, her hands slathered with soap, she again summoned Lady McB and spoke her words:

"Out, damned spot! out I say!—One: two: why, then, 'tis time to do't.—Hell is murky!—Fie, my

lord, fie! a soldier, and afeard? What need we
fear who knows it, when non can call our power to
account?"

She ran her hands under the water, turned it off with
her elbow and took out a clean cup towel. She wiped
her face and dried her hands.

Holding the cup towel she took the lid off the cookie
jar.

Again, she froze. She looked around. Barbeque tongs
stuck up from a fat ceramic canister that matched the
fat cookie jar, both inherited from her grandmother,
both adorned with tiny purple hyssop flowers, symbols
of purification. She grabbed the tongs with the towel
and peered into the cookie jar.

She pulled out a one-dollar bill. It dangled at the end
of the tongs like limp lettuce.

She stopped, staring at the dollar bill.

You can do this. Money across the palm like before.

She reached toward the dollar to stroke it across her
palm. She would feel better.

But she stopped, her hand in the air, her chest
pounding, sweat gathering on her face, the back of her
neck.

They were there again. The vermin. Crawling across
the dollar like demons. Millions of tiny pathogens
multiplying like in the Petri dish. Overflowing onto the
table, filling the biology lab.

She closed her eyes.

*No, no, no, no! Don't do this, you brain-dead phobia. Do
not take this from me, you jealous bitch,* she thought.

She started to shake, the dollar bill at the end of the tongs jerking like a dead animal. She shook her head and the tongs and the bill fell to the ground.

"Damn you, phobia. I will not let you ruin my life again." She grabbed a saucepan, filled it with water, and put it on the stove. She turned the burner on high.

Blue flames flared up.

She stared at the beautiful blue, cleansing flames licking the pot, its copper bottom darkening. Flames blue as the veins rippling across her Granny's hands, bruised and blackened and dying there among the tubes and needles they said would keep her alive, the liars.

Liars. They were all liars, she thought.

She looked at the photo of her mother. "You lied, Mama," she said. "A little dirt can kill somebody. Granny got sick and weak. Too weak to eat. Too weak to go to church. Too weak to pray. Granny couldn't even pray, Mama. She couldn't even hold her beloved hyssop flowers to cleanse herself from whatever piddly sins she thought she had."

"'Purge me with hyssop, and I shall be clean,' she used to say, remember? She was too weak to smell her flowers, and she was damn sure too weak to fight off the germs. Those little buggers you said were harmless."

"Granny died, Mama. Those 'harmless' little buggers killed her."

Don't you understand? she had wanted to shout to her mother at her Granny's funeral. *My little buggers killed her. I brought my sweaty adolescent germs into her room. It was all my fault Granny died with her sins uncleansed.*

"Repent thy wickedness!" the preacher had said at the funeral. He was talking to her. Her wicked germs had killed her granny. She'd seen them under the microscope. Thousands of them. Everywhere. On her hands, her hair. Grotesque, predatory little buggers ready to attack. She had to make sure it would not happen again. Not to her or her mother or anyone.

She turned back to the stove and watched the fire dance under the pot. Her hands began to flicker in unison. The water began to boil, roiling and bubbling like an angry sea god avenging her grandmother's death.

"God is a consuming fire," she remembered the preacher saying. It had comforted her then and it comforted her now.

She smiled. *I will make it right, Granny,* she thought. *I will make them pay, the predatory little buggers that took you from me.*

She grabbed the towel and picked up the dollar bill with the tongs.

"Take that," she whispered as she plunged the dollar bill into the boiling water. Instantly, it began to undulate, rising and falling in spasms, the placid face of George Washington gurgling among the bubbles.

"Die, you evil buggers," she said. "You pestilence, you pox."

Boil their bodies. Dissolve their insides. Let them scream with their invisible mouths. See if I care.

"Boil, buggers, boil," she whispered, and she started to laugh.

A deep, uncontrollable laugh came from some dark place inside her. She collapsed on the linoleum and started to cry. Huge, gasping sobs like convulsions.

I can't do this again, she thought. *I can't go back. I can't. Save me. Oh Lord, save me.*

Above her, steam billowed from the pot.

Finally, she stopped. She sat spent and panting on the floor until her breath slowed; then she reached up and turned off the burner, the blue flames disappearing.

She stood and watched the water grow still, the dollar bill slowly settling to the bottom of the pan. The dead microbes dissolving, disappearing back into whatever evil place they came from.

She fished out the dollar bill with the tongs. She pulled out a fresh towel, laid the wet dollar bill on top, and blotted it.

She inhaled and placed the dollar bill in her hand.

She stroked it once across George Washington's face.

Then once across the one-eyed pyramid on the back.

And finally, across the Treasury seal on the front.

And there it was again, the sweet release of equilibrium, all the mitochondria in her body suddenly able to breathe again.

Respiration.

Respite.

Redemption.

You didn't kill her, girl. You didn't. Your Granny was just too sick.

She slid down and sat on the floor, holding the one dollar like a newborn babe.

She closed her eyes and felt her Granny come to her, wrapping her arms around her again and stroking her hair. "It's all right, child," her granny said, and finally it was. *All better.*

All better.

All better.

"Caminante, no hay camino. Se hace camino al andar."
Antonio Machado

Votive Candle

One dollar Australian only buys Barb one votive candle, or so goes the unspoken rule of the chapel according to the other tourists in the Colombian *zócalo*, the price ticking up over the years since her church group's visit here a decade past, like a celestial prime rate set by the archangels of inflation.

In the darkened alcove for Santa Barbara, a sprinkling of votive candles blazes, the source flame nestled in the belly of Barb's patron saint, the fire within a white-hot glow of destruction, desire, rage, rebirth. Fallen away Catholic though she is, Barb fancies lighting all the votive candles, a crowd of fiery lights all bending God's ear in her favor, sensing in her gut that she will need her namesake saint Santa Barbara in saving her from *El Guapetón*.

But one defunct Australian dollar note, a souvenir Rooboy, is all she's willing to wager, heathen that she is now, so she folds it neatly like the indigenous girls fold the sun-dried bed sheets in the pensión above Bogotá. She doubles its worthless paper over three times and presses the bill into the brass box that holds the treasures of dreamers and daughters and thieves.

"Please, *por favor, mi Santa Sagrada,*" she mutters, mimicking the voices of the village girls praying to their sacred saints at their altar in the barren dirt of their courtyard.

The votive candles beckon.

"Por favor," Barb says, haunted by the triple-bagged cocaine pellets—*las pepas*—heavy inside her belly. She falls to her knees in sudden contrition now. Her fear deepens, her thoughts rush: *please, please,* she prays, *just let me get through this.* She fumbles in her bag for a newer Aussie dollar coin to drop into the votive box but finds none. She bows her head, felled as she's been by the lure of quick money and adventure. She clasps her hands and presses them against her forehead—a reluctant penitent—her skin damp with the dread of the cold hard gaze of security agents soon to be upon her.

She is inextricably bound now into service to *El Guapetón,* the handsome one, the dashing local handler for the other tourist drug mules they'd met at the club, she and her girlfriends with their heads spinning with margaritas and blow, bedazzled by his charms, these fading gringas out for a last lark of their twenties, a final walk on the wild side to reminisce about when they are old. Fallen Catholics, fallen women, easy marks.

Outside the chapel the airport taxi sounds. Her reckoning awaits.

"Por favor, Santa Barbara," Barb whispers to the saint chosen for her by her family so many years ago. Patron saint of sudden death, of tempests, soldiers, beheaded daughters. Her forgotten faith calls to her and she leans toward it in earnest now, wondering if they had known then, her family, that she would come to this, pleading with her patron saint to save her? Like Santa Barbara, she too is an only daughter and still unwed, still turning her heart hard against the sweet young men who'd come calling in her father's house. Like Santa Barbara she too fled, out of the confines of her west Australian town into the wild world unknown. But their paths, hers and her saint's, thenceforth parted.

Trembling, Barb touches the lighting taper to the flame and, watching it burst alive, lights her votive candle for the blessed Santa Barbara. It glimmers and dances, this relic of conquistadores, protecting her, perhaps, perhaps not, as Santa Barbara's history tumbles back to her.

Santa Barbara the Martyr betrayed her pagan father and fell in love with Jesus. Virginity and piety and humility enveloped her, and her father raged. She fled into the hills opened for her by divine command. And there she hid until a shepherd revealed her. Captured and beaten and starved, dragged naked through the streets of her father's pagan city, burned with torches, still she did not denounce her Lord. Jesus healed her wounds and the unfallen angels clothed and shielded her, and again her father raged. He drew his sword and beheaded her, his only daughter, the virgin, the Christian, and still unwed. Her martyred head, bleeding and beautiful, lay still upon the ground.

There, alone in a chapel ten thousand miles from home, Barb weeps for the once sweet child of Santa Barbara she was and can be no longer, the innocent girl, child of Christ, beloved by all, gone. What had become of her mother's child? Her father's angel? *"Por favor,"* she murmurs, praying to her namesake for deliverance, a second chance at choosing. She grips the wood of the prayer stand, the *prie-dieu, el reclinatorio* worn smooth with a land's lamentations of five hundred years. *Wanderer, there is no path,* the shadows say. *The path is made by walking.*

Suddenly, blinding white pain surges through her. Spasms knock her to the ground and pound her head against the stones of the ancients. She grows cold, a deep blue engulfs her. Her eyes roll back, and the blessed Santa Barbara comes to her, naked, emaciated. *Por favor, Santa Barbara,* her vision cries, and the faces of hacienda girls appear. *Por favor, Santa Barbara,* they cry, and the blessed saint's pagan father brandishes his sword. His face melts into the smiling face of *El Guapetón,* the vanquisher. The martyred blood of Santa Barbara drips from his chin. Flames lick at Santa Barbara's conquered torso. The mouth of *El Guapetón* opens and severed heads roll out, one head, two heads, three heads, four.

Their tongues black, their eyes a crystal white, they roll toward her, speaking Barbara's name, her invitation to a beheading.

Death calls to Barb, as it called to Santa Barbara, and the beheaded bodies of village girls float before her, their bellies filled with desperation. Beasts of burden, the walking dead, bearing death in their entrails, their bodies twitching as Barb's body twitches.

Falling, she is falling, a black fog closing, closing, closing, until at last all is darkness.

There, in a chapel on a hillside over Bogotá, a votive candle of the virgin Santa Barbara, martyr of Christendom, burns. The blessings of one discontinued dollar flick a lonely tongue beside the small, still body of young Barbara, ten thousand miles from home.

Bloody Rabbit

One dollar. That's all he wanted, the still-trembling boy with the black rabbit bloody in his hands. A baby rabbit so black its blood shown only on the small pale hands of the boy.

"One dollar." The boy smiled at her. "For da rabbit," he said in a Balkan accent thick with purpose.

Too young for death, she thought. *The rabbit. Oh, and the boy. He's too young for death as well.* Like everyone in this war-torn place the global technology foundation had decided they should visit for reasons that seemed apocalyptic to her now. All of them, the people here and even the anemic cows in the field, waded in death like fishermen hauling in their nets. Especially the old women, the thousand-year-old-looking women whose suffering seemed to hold all life together. They wallowed in death; it was the air they breathed and the phlegm they spat out at her and her colleagues as they passed. It was suffocating.

Get me out of here, she thought.

"One dollar," the boy shouted again at the group of them, the visitors, salesmen really, opportunists, their translators whispered, come from realities far away, bringing their technology with them. Magic elixirs—they touted them as panaceas for devastation, these modern digital devices their group waved before the battered local officials like the boy was waving the dead rabbit.

"One dollar buy one rabbit." The boy stepped toward her. The blood slid further down his arms.

She stepped back and the boy stopped. They looked at each other. She glanced at her colleagues, but she was the only one watching the boy.

"One dollar disemboweled," the boy added, keeping his distance now and gesturing at the underbelly of the baby rabbit.

Disemboweled? She marveled at the word. *How does a boy here among the illiterate rabble learn a word like disemboweled?*

In her peripheral vision she saw her colleagues—all men—glance at their watches and inch back toward their hired cars and drivers. The technology foundation had spared no expense in their quest for reconstruction dollars. The men regarded the boy from a distance, holding their tongues and averting their eyes like the enlightened travelers they fancied themselves to be.

The boy too saw the visitors' retreat. "One dollar," he shouted, again moving toward the men, swinging the dead rabbit before them like a bloody flag of surrender.

Poor boy, she thought. *Does he really think we will buy his bloody rabbit? Who does he think we are?*

Her colleagues were now openly retreating away from the boy. Everyone on the global vanguard sales team moving from discreet withdrawal toward flight mode.

$

An adventurous getaway to the boundary lands, they'd told their consorts. This far-flung place would be in bloom this time of year, their ex-pat colleagues had said, before the rains come and all hope turns to mud and pathogens. And besides, the tech foundation will pay for everything.

$

The boy, looking defeated, turned and fixed his gaze on her, the lone woman in this swell of pompous men. "One dollar?" He stretched out his hand toward her, bloody palm side up like a beggar.

The dead rabbit hung limp behind him.

She reached into the compartment hidden beneath her waistband and slid out one dollar American to give to the boy.

"One dollar," she said, smiling. "For you, young man."

The boy snatched the dollar from her hand and thrust the rabbit toward her.

"Oh no," she said. "A gift. You can keep your rabbit."

The boy cradled the dead baby rabbit in both hands and looked at her.

What a sweet child, she thought.

And then the boy, muttering something, leaned forward on one foot and hurled the dripping rabbit at her feet. Blood and sinews splattered up, covering the white calf-skin boots she'd bought only that morning at the hotel boutique.

"One dollar for one rabbit," the boy shouted and ran away.

Gathered Loved Ones

Mashed Potatoes

"One dollar says you won't do it," Gracie said.

"Will too," I answered. What else could I have said back then?

"Mama will kill us," Gracie warned.

"She will not."

"You ain't never seen my mama mad." Gracie cocked her head forward and looked at me through her bangs.

"I know. But she won't kill us."

"So, you'll do it?"

"Sure I will," I said, even though I knew betting against Gracie was a dumb idea. Even back in kindergarten I'd figured out that doing anything against Gracie was doomed to fail. I knew that, of course, but back in the heat of July, the bet was on.

"You mean it?" Gracie poked her chin in the air.

"Will your mama make me eat peas?" I asked.

"Nah, Mama don't care nothing about you eating no peas. She likes you, Brenda. When did she ever make you eat peas?"

"Then I'll do it."

"Promise?"

"Yeah, promise."

"It's a bet then. First one finishes slinging their mashed potatoes wins the war."

"Gracie?"

"Yeah?"

"No eating the mashed potatoes, right? That's against the rules, right?"

"Right. No eating allowed."

And so, what years later we called the "The Great Mashed Potato War of 1964" was on.

Gracie plopped the jumbo blue bowl of her mother's best, whole-milk, real-butter, smooth-as-Ponds-cold-cream leftover mashed potatoes in front of me and handed me the two biggish bowls we ate cereal out of most of the time.

"Divvy it up, Brenda," Gracie said. "Equal parts for you and me."

I thought about that years later. "Equal parts for you and me," and how it hadn't worked out that way, but I didn't know that then. Back then, I only knew I loved Gracie. That she was what made my life one long string of adventures I never would have had without her and how much I owed her for that.

"You ready?" Gracie said when I handed her the two bowls piled high with cold, creamy mashed potatoes and the two spoons we'd used that very morning to shovel Sugar Pops in our mouths in front of Saturday morning cartoons.

At the count of three Gracie set the two bowls in the middle of the kitchen floor between us, and we'd gone at each other like chimpanzees on a rampage.

Gracie hit me between the eyes, and I retaliated with a glob on Gracie's grin. An overhand spoonful hit me in the chest, and an underhand hurl clobbered Gracie on the butt. Gracie took position on top of the double sink, pulling her mama's ruffled kitchen curtain in front of her for protection, and I hid behind the Mixmaster from whence the mashed weaponry had come a day before. On and on The Great Mashed Potato War raged until all the potatoes were gone, and we and the kitchen and everything in it was pockmarked like pancake batter ready to be flipped.

I could never in a thousand years have ever, ever done this in my own mama's kitchen. The halls of propriety would have come tumbling, crashing, exploding down, and my calm, lean Yankee mama would have screeched the screech I always knew she had in her.

I didn't really think that we could do this in Gracie's mama's kitchen either, even though it was Gracie's idea and, like I said, I didn't argue with Gracie. Not ever. I didn't really argue with anyone back then. Arguing, heck, even speaking in public outside my house or Gracie's house or once or twice at Sunday School was way, way beyond me. Giggle, yes, I giggled a lot at stuff the other fifth graders did or said.

But mostly I just laughed with Gracie, great, deep, fall-over belly laughs. Like when we'd sneak into the

Bayou Drive-In Movie Theater in the trunk of Gracie's mama's car, me curled up in the well for the spare tire that Gracie's sisters had taken out to make room for us, annoying as we were. I'd curl up inside the hole with my feet sticking up in Gracie's face and she would start tickling my toes between my flip-flops just when we got to the ticket gate, and I would bite down hard on my plastic oval money case that looked like flattened Silly Putty with my one and only dollar inside, trying not to laugh and get us all in trouble. And then Gracie's mama would park and open the trunk, and Gracie and I would bust open laughing and fall out of the trunk onto the ground, and I'd be so happy I'd blow my whole dollar buying us both jumbo Milk Duds from the concession stand.

Turned out, I'd been right all along. We really couldn't wage a Great Mashed Potato War in Gracie's mama's kitchen after all. Not after she got home.

It took us all night to scrub the floors and walls and countertops, and weeks of extra chores at Gracie's house or my house that had nothing to do with the Mashed Potato War, but we finally got back to the business of summer right before the fall came and our last year of elementary school began. By holiday time all was forgiven, and everything was once more right with the world.

When the Christmas season came Gracie's mama was cooking peas again, winking at me one cool December night 'cause she knew I still didn't like peas. Didn't like the way they popped open in my mouth and mushed green all over my tongue. But big green peas were Gracie's daddy's favorite, and for once he was home from the high seas, a Merchant Marine on holiday, and so big green peas it was.

Peas and mashed potatoes.

The soft, smooth mound of Idaho's Finest were piled high that night in Gracie's mama's best serving bowl next to the Wonder Bread and Heinz Ketchup on the table in front of Gracie's daddy. I took a heaping spoonful and plopped it steaming on my plate. I'd always loved mashed potatoes, even before the famous Mashed Potato War. I loved the way you could create a crater lake in the middle and melt a whole wad of butter inside it and then make little breaks in the crater with the side of your fork and watch the melted butter flow down like golden lava and spread out over the turquoise Fiesta Ware Gracie's grandmamma had brought from Mobile, Alabama before she died.

I made a perfect, smooth little crater in my potatoes, more like an empty birdbath really than a real lake but no matter. I nudged Gracie to pass the butter, then took a long swig of sweet tea, so sweet it made my head pound a little. Gracie picked up the butter plate and handed it to me, but then she wouldn't let go. I looked at her and she smiled her big toothy smile and let mashed potatoes ooze out between her teeth, and I practically choked right then and there trying not to spew sweet tea all over Gracie's mother's dinner table all nice with its red-flowered tablecloth.

Gracie's daddy grinned at us and tilted his head and crossed his eyes and stuck out his tongue. Gracie and I cracked up all over again and even Gracie's mama laughed her deep belly laugh; Gracie's sisters just looked at each other and shook their heads and muttered "juvenile" under their breath, but no one noticed.

Gracie's mother passed them the meatloaf and they both took a slice. Gracie pounded on the bottom of the glass Heinz bottle and some more ketchup plopped out onto her meatloaf. Then she plopped some more on mine too. I took a big bite—I loved Gracie's mama's meatloaf with its sweet layer of baked ketchup on top like cherry icing—and was just about to dive into my mashed potato mountain when Gracie's daddy began to cough a kind of low, goosey, honking cough. He grabbed his chest and slumped across the table, knocking the salt and pepper shakers over, and flecks of white and gray trickled out.

Gracie's mother turned ashen, and she jumped up and rushed to her husband's side at the head of the kitchen table. She felt his head and grabbed his shoulders and started screaming and shaking him. Someone, most likely Gracie's older sister, grabbed the phone on the wall and called for help.

Everything else blurred together. Suddenly, there were flashing lights and ambulance men rushing in. My mama appeared and somehow got Gracie and me back down the street to our house where my daddy was on the phone.

He took off his glasses and nodded once, then hung up the phone and leaned and whispered to my mama, who closed her eyes and shook her head before pulling me and Gracie to her and giving us a long and silent hug.

Gracie couldn't stop pacing that night, swinging her skinny arms across her chest, flat as it was still on the brink of adolescence. My mama helped us build a fire in the fireplace and make up beds with blankets and a couple of my granny's crocheted Afghans in front of the fireplace in the living room. My mama brought us two pairs of flannel pajamas, but Gracie said she didn't want to change just in case, so I said I didn't either, and my mama put the PJs down and let us have the living room to ourselves.

Gracie finally sat down in front of the fire, and I went to the kitchen and got two long barbeque forks and some marshmallows and sat there toasting marshmallows for us both, but Gracie didn't want to eat anything, and it was the only time I could remember since we'd started being best friends in kindergarten, that Gracie didn't have anything to say at all.

I just sat there roasting marshmallows and letting the soft blobs of sugar turn brown and crispy on the outside and was sliding them off onto the plastic picnic plate I'd picked up from the kitchen when Gracie started to cry, big sucking sobs like the vacuum cleaner at a car wash.

My mama came rushing in with more blankets and a glass of water, but I just pulled Gracie to me and rocked her back and forth the way my mama did when I woke up frightened in the night. My mama sat down on one of the straight-backed chairs at the dining room table and watched us for a time, then she left us alone.

Gracie and I sat there rocking like that, still in our clothes, the fireplace fire burning down and the crispy marshmallows flattening like melting scoops of ice cream until Gracie stopped sobbing and just sat there next to me.

I pulled a blanket over us and reached into my pocket. "Here," I said and held out a wrinkled dollar bill.

Gracie looked at me in confusion.

"I never paid up on our bet last summer, but I figure you won the Great Mashed Potato War hands down, so here you go," I said.

"Keep it," Gracie said, running her shirt sleeve over her face. "I'd say it was a draw."

And with that Gracie pulled her knees up under her chin and wrapped her arms around her legs and put her head down and closed her eyes.

I sat there watching her pull into herself, and for the first time the fearless Gracie I would have followed anywhere, Gracie who was so much stronger and taller and more beautiful than me, looked small and frail and frightened. I took the blanket off my shoulders and wrapped it around her.

I stuffed the dollar back in my pocket and reached for one of the Afghans my granny had crocheted. I pulled it up under my chin and closed my eyes and cried.

Festus

Aon dhuillear

Gavin MacFarlane, Attorney at Law, glanced at the Gaelic words scrawled across the bottom of the document and knew that this would not end well. *Oh, my lord*, he thought, as the mother tongue of his Scottish grandmother came flooding back to him. He looked up at old man Buchanan's family, gathered in dribs and drabs across the veranda in the unbending Oklahoma heat. Who knew that the old man had this many kin, living alone as he had all these years out on the homestead with only that bum-legged old Mexican man to help him. *Joaquin*, the lawyer thought, *I think that's his name.*

From across the pasture the bull brayed, the last of the old man's herd, ill-mannered and ornery like the old man was, a sour old coot nobody, not even a milk cow in heat, could abide anymore.

The lawyer loosened his tie and cleared his throat. *Read the will and be gone*, he thought.

The youngest children squirmed in their mamas' laps, and the women shushed them with a righteous slap.

"Ladies and Gentlemen, Gathered Loved Ones." Mr. MacFarlane peered across the veranda and smiled. The menfolk in back, leaning against the rail, stopped talking and stood upright. "The unfortunate mishap of your loved one's accident," the lawyer pointed to the old bull in the corner of the pasture, "at the hands of his prized bull ..."

"Festus," shouted a little girl wedged between two older sisters on the porch swing.

"Excuse me?" asked the lawyer.

"Festus, that's the bull's name," said the girl. "It means faithful friend."

"Oh," said MacFarlane. "Yes, of course. Your loved one's unfortunate impaling by Festus," he nodded at the young girl, and she smiled back at him, "has brought us here on this sorrowful day for the reading of his last will and testament. Thank you for making the journey out here."

An old woman sitting on the wicker rocker coughed. The rocker creaked as she leaned forward and spit over the railing.

"Well, let me get right to it." The lawyer opened his collar wider.

"'I, Horace Angus Buchanan, being of sound mind and body, do hereby bequeath to my entire family,'" Gavin MacFarlane, Esq., suddenly turned a dismal shade of pale. He took a deep breath and read on. "'... to my entire family ... putrid, unrepentant swine that they are ...'"

A murmur fluttered across the porch. MacFarlane held up the document. "Forgive my language, ladies, but that's exactly what it says here. I am sorry for the unpleasantness. '... do hereby bequeath to my entire family ... the grand old sum of *aon dhuillear.*'"

MacFarlane paused and took in the uncomprehending gazes upon him. "To continue reading, folks, Mr. Buchanan explains right here, though there's more unpleasantness I'm afraid ... 'that's one dollar to all you ignorant fools who forgot where you come from. Now, you scallywags can fight amongst yourselves for a lousy buck.'"

A collective gasp rose from the veranda.

"'The remainder of my estate,'" MacFarlane continued, eager to get it over with, "'I leave to Joaquin Morales for the care and feeding of the prize bull named Festus, my one and only friend, for the rest of its earth-bound days. Signed, Horace Angus Buchanan, the soon-to-be deceased son of bitch ain't none of you jackasses troubled yourselves with for going on fifty years now.'"

Gavin MacFarlane, Esq., stopped. In the silence he folded the yellowed document and put it back in its manila envelope.

One of the mamas with a young one started to cry, then another youngster started to cry, and then all the babies were crying, and from the back of the veranda, the menfolk started cussing.

"Crazy old fart," muttered a tall, skinny fellow with mud on his boots.

"Damn him and his mean ass bull," said another under his breath.

"I'll be a son of a gun, ain't that the shits," said a third and laughed a bitter laugh.

"What the hell we supposed to do now, Mr. Fancy Citified Lawyer Man, huh?" another man with a scraggly gray beard shouted, and the men stared at MacFarlane.

Time to find Joaquin Morales, MacFarlane thought, and throwing a weak smile to the menfolk, he hustled over to his 1927 Ford Model A and started it up.

Out in the field, Festus stomped. He shook his horns and bellowed.

The old woman in the rocker slowly pulled herself up. She leaned over and the hem of her dress brushed across the silvered planks of the veranda.

"*Aon dhuiller,* my ass." She unhooked the Winchester rifle that old man Buchanan always kept strapped to the back of his rocker. And as she headed for Festus in the field, a swirl of dust billowed behind her in the epic Oklahoma wind.

Aunt Shirley

One dollar dangled from Shirley's hand. "Damn," she said as she leaned over a gnarled Japanese Red Pine in a porcelain planter at the Bonsai Pavilion of the National Arboretum. "These trees are older than shit."

She folded the dollar bill into a paper airplane and zoomed it over to my seven-year-old daughter Fiona, who ran giggling after it.

"Fly that baby buck over yonder, Peanut." Shirley pointed to the donation box.

"Hell, let's give them two dollars." She pressed another bill into airplane form and zipped it past the head of my four-year-old son Liam clamoring over the boulders nearby. "Over there, Cowboy," she said. "See if you can fly that buckaroo into that little box there, Buddy."

While the kids vied with each other trying to fly their dollars into the donation box, I examined the sign on the Bonsai tree. *Pinus densiflora,* it said. *In training since 1795. Donated by The Imperial Household, 1975.*

"Good God," I said. "This tree is over two hundred years old."

"Yeah," said Shirley. "These buggers are off the hook, huh?" She bent and examined the wires wound like primal chains around the trunk of this miniature pine.

I reached for the brochure. "Listen to this, kiddos," I said, clearing my throat. "'In the Japanese art of bonsai, woody plants in containers are pruned and their branches are shaped using wire to give the impression of ancient trees.'"

The Japanese Red Pine sat, dignified, before me. "'This art form dates back to about the sixth century BCE,'" I read to the tree, "'and is derived from an ancient Chinese horticultural practice, part of which was then redeveloped under the influence of Japanese Zen Buddhism.'"

Liam darted past me, then froze and struck one of his many super-hero poses, right arm out, his fingers pinching an invisible arrow, his left arm back, stretching his invisible bow.

"Hey Shirley, listen to this." I put my hands up in mock surrender to Liam's stance. "'Tree binding is an ancient art practiced on living things that will outlive the artist.'"

Shirley raised one eyebrow the way she had as a kid and tickled Fiona, who was placing one sneakered foot in front of the other, ballerina arms out, along the low stone wall beside the walkway on a sneak approach to the paper airplane game. Fiona squealed and threw herself into my friend's arms and tickled her Aunt Shirley back under her long arms that floated like tree branches from her tall, slim body.

"'Bonsai artists.'" I turned to Liam, who now swung monkey-boy-like on the low railing with his dollar airplane in his mouth. "Yo, Liam," I said. "Check this out. 'Bonsai artists pass on their botanical charges to younger practitioners who, through the ravages of history, find sanctuary for the trees.'"

Liam skipped from stone to stone on the pathway toward Shirley where she snatched his dollar and zoomed it perfectly into the donation box.

I put the brochure back in my pocket and looked around. Nearly a hundred of these tiny trees resided there—at the Arboretum, this cloistered, pastoral place just yards from the afflicted DC streets, filled with hookers and hustlers and old men with grocery carts crammed with crushed aluminum.

Across the pavilion Shirley, the kid whisperer, trotted Fiona piggyback to slam dunk her dollar into the box. They loped back toward Liam, who'd shimmied his small body up the metal gate. Liam hung there screeching with delight as Shirley and Fiona swung the gate back and forth like cards shuffling in the Game of Shirley.

The Game of Shirley had been the instructional manual of my childhood.

$

After a lull of decades when we'd both moved away and had our separate loves and lives, Shirley and I had become close again when we were both in our small

Southern hometown for a time. She'd moved back home to battle breast cancer and I had stayed home for a few months to help my dad after my mother's sudden death.

When I saw Shirley then after her surgery and chemo, her chest was flat again, the way it had been when we'd met in kindergarten. The way it was when, even at five years old, she—the leader of the wild kid pack—had taken me underwing. Me, this this paralyzingly shy kid who didn't speak in public until I was sixteen. But for the whole of my childhood, it didn't matter because when I was with Shirley, which was always, I *belonged*. There was no loneliness, no uncertainty, no grappling with my place in the world.

When I was with Shirley, I was part of something much larger than myself, something larger even than friendship. Shirley was a feat of nature. She was a grand story, and she had written me into it. Like the Bonsai Tree artist, she had given me sanctuary through the ravages of my brief history. It was *magic*.

I was her constant sidekick, lapping milk out of bowls on the floor pretending we were dogs, chasing horses in the field, floating down the Prairie Branch Creek in a kiddie wading pool, riding our bikes down the underside of the one overpass in town, breaking into Seaside Nursery with the bad boys to drive the little tractors around, stealing makeup from Woolworths, smoking cigarettes in the tool shed, and on and on until puberty hit and suddenly we were riding around in cars with older boys who lusted after young girls like Shirley; until everything changed, and the adventures weren't just kid stuff and I knew we couldn't be best friends anymore, and I lost my place the world for a time.

Shirley is long gone now, her unbridled, kid-whispering aliveness no longer taking kiddos like me and my children underwing and showing them how to take life by the lapels and shake it and shake it until it loosened its tie and took off its shoes and boogied on down to the dance floor with her.

My children are grown now with intricately woven lives of their own, but we still come to see the tiny Bonsai Trees when they visit with their own children.

"Give them a baby buck, Peanut," I say to my grandchildren, relishing one of Shirley's vast store of pet names as I fold a bill into an airplane shape. "Hell, let's give them two dollars, Cowboy." I press another airplaned dollar bill into my grandson's hands.

The grandkids zoom their dollar airplanes into the same donation box with the same earnest intent their parents had so long ago, enchanted by their Aunt Shirley.

I lean again into the tiny tree before me, the echo of my indomitable best friend reverberating, and suddenly I feel a rush of kinship with the Bonsai Tree, for I, like it, have been permanently shaped by one whose ancient art on living things outlived the artist.

Amygdala-la-la-la

"One dollar!" Babs be shouting, waking me up. *God fucking damnit. Here I was all dope dreamy and shit, not thinking about them motherfuckers watching us all the time. Pointing them rusty ass gats at you, telling you to get the fuck away from the wall or they gonna smash your fucking face in. Cocksuckers. I'd like to smash them into the fucking ground, rub their stink ass faces into the rubble and slice their eyes with the damn razor wire they got strung all over the goddamn place.*

"Yo, Mazy. One dollar!" Babs shouting again.

"Say what? What you see, girl?"

Oh shit. Babs bouncing again, rocking to the rhythm of her own sweet beat.

"Spot that dollar, yo, little snatch of dollar," she say.

Babs be pointing to a little piece of dollar sticking out of a pile of crap, busted-up bricks and concrete and shit. *Like the whole rest of this hell hole.*

"Woo, baby," I say to Babs 'cause she got fucking radar, man. "You got game, girl. Eagle fuckin' eyes. Old-time dollar! For our co-llec-tion!" I say 'cause we got a fucking collection—every piece of money you can think of, we got it. Been collecting it, smoothing it out and keeping it fine. *It so fine, man. Pretty to look at and sweet to the touch.*

"Old timey dollar, way over yonder. In the rubble and the trouble and the double decay." Babs singing.

I look closer, digging the way Babs can spot a dollar from way over yonder.

"Heh, hey. Go lizard brain." Babs tripping now. "Lizzy, lizzy, lizzy brain. Rockin' amyg-da-la-la-la. Zip, zap. Quickedy quick."

"Slide your butt over," I say to Babs.

But then them motherfuckers on the wall come back, waving their rickety Uzis around, shouting at us rabble.

"Shhh," I say. "Wait."

Babs stops tripping. She cool.

"Freeze," I say. "Don't let them see you, girl. Motherfuckers. Steal your shit. Bust your head flat open. Take our fucking collection and leave us dead."

Fuck. Makes me mad just thinking about them cocksuckers, think they got it over us leftovers just 'cause they got some punk ass rusty nines and we nothings got nothing.

"Slow, baby, ice slo-o-o-o-w," I tell Babs nice and low-like and she sliding over toward the rubble nice and slow like. "Now slide your hand over," I tell her. "Slide it under da money."

Babs got her hand under it now and she riffing again.

"That old-time money." Babs singing, her voice all highty high. "Just a comin' round to me."

"That's right," I say, "That old-money, honey."

Babs got her hand, all rosy pink, under the rubble now and she snatch that dollar and zap it back under them covers.

"Ha, Mazy! Got it! Got it, got it, got it." Babs shouting.

"Shh! Now, crunch it up," I tell her. "Slow now. Make a fist."

Babs done scoot her butt back over here now, still singing all low-like.

"Found me a trampled, tattered, rotted baby buck, Mazy." She rocking slow, singing. "Got us da money, honey. Da old-time money."

"Oh Shit. Quit your singing, girl," I tell Babs. "Fucking assholes are back, bitch barking again. Shhh! Close your eyes. Fake them out. Play possum."

Babs done froze. *Damn, she cool.*

"Play that possum. Old woman done died."

"What the fuck. Quit your singing, girl. Be still. We be nothing." Them punks be looking again.

"Old baby don't cry," Babs say real low.

"Hush!" I tell her but she got me thinking. "Hey, what's that from?" I ask.

"Oh baby don't cry." Bab start rocking all slow-like.

"Ah, fuck it. OK, we ain't crying. Look around, Babs. They gone?"

"They gone, baby. The rabble, the riff-raff, the no good, no count, dummy scummy bum bums." Babs be looking, looking.

"Damn. You crack me up, Babs. You right though. They gone. All the hoity-toity fat cats gone. All the kumbaya gone. All the what-the-fucks gone. We riff-raff's only ones left alive."

"After the fall, baby." *Oh Lord, Babs testifying now.* "After the hollow, hollow, hollow-caust," she be saying.

"True dat, Babs. Fuckin' holocaust."

"*Kaboom! Kwish! Pwshew!* All gone." Babs be 'sploding now. Her hands be poppin'.

"Girl, you right. Ain't nothing left but us rabble."

"*Zap, zap, zap.*" Babs zapping now.

"OK, coast is clear, baby. Lemme get the collection. We got the box, the big red box all snuggly in the bag. Ain't gonna let them punk ass shitheads take the collection. Ain't worth shit but it's fucking beautiful, man."

"Beauty, beauty, beautiful," Babs say.

"You did it, Babs," I tell her. "You got the dollar. Add it to our collection. Can't nobody beat our collection. We got all the coins of the realm."

"Uh huh, uh huh, I'm in the money, now."

"Come on, girl. Let's see what we got." It be risky I know, looking over the collection in the light but I got to see it now. "Oh sugar, look at this," I tell Babs and she pull the blanket over top and we looking all quiet-like. "Here, smooth them out," I say. "That's right. Let's stack them up. A mountain of treasure. All the fuckin' coins in the realm, yo!"

"Honey, honey money. Dat's what I like! My Mazy Maz."

"You got that right!" I say to Babs. "Man, look at all this treasure. We got the fucking five-dollar red seal, baby. And the ten-spot from Fort fricking Worth, and the twenty from WMDC. Oh, and here's our fifty, and big mama hundred, signed by Rosa Rosa Rio, whoever that was."

"Got us da money ..."

"Shhh. Yo Babs, look at this here baby. Quiet now. This be the queen. The thousand-dollar queen! Woo mama, look at that. Ain't she pretty!"

"Queeny weeny. You be pretty." Babs cooing at the queen.

"That's right, girl. You sing it. Don't be kissin' it now. We got to keep the queen sanctified!"

"Queen of the baby dollars." Babs be stroking it now, all gentle-like.

"Hey lemme see that new baby dollar. Damn, it's pretty too. Shit, girl, you got some eagle fuckin' eyes. Done spot that fucker way over yonder. Just a little peeky peek sticking out."

Oh god, here come Babs rocking again. "Amyg-da-fuckin'-la-la-la." She rocking. "Little lizard brain still got game. Uh huh, uh huh, uh huh!"

"Man, how'd you do that?" I ask Babs. "Damn, like X-ray vision, baby. Like magic fuckin' power."

Now Babs be pounding air. *She a fighter, yo.*

"Zip zap the power," Babs saying. "Zip zap the power. Lizard Brain power. Like the Brain Man said." She be zippin'. I be zappin'.

"Yeah, back in the backday, brothers and sisters," I tell Babs. "Dr. Brain Man got the score." I be pointing. Babs be nodding.

"Got the scoop, Mazy," Babs saying. "Got the 411. Back in the back day, baby, when da moon was in the heaven's hallelujah."

"Man," I tell Babs. "Dr. Brain Man could preach the preach of the mighty amygdala-la-la-la. Instant fuckin' action, y'all. *Mmm ... mmm.* Gonna love me some amgy-dala-la-la. Mr. Professor, you da man, yo." I be smacking my lips.

"Yo yo mama. Mazy Maz. Daddy brain man be cookin'. Lizard brain be lookin' and lookie, lookie here."

Babs done toss off the blanket and she be waving the new dollar 'round now.

"A risket a rasket, got money in my basket," she taunting.

"Ha! Shit. Wait a minute. Get your hand down, Babs." *Them motherfuckers gonna see us and bust us up.* "Don't wave it around," I tell her. "Them SOBs gonna see it."

"Na, na, na, na, na, na!" *Damn,* Babs be waving.

"Jesus Fucking Christ. Quit waving that sucker, Babs." I grab Babs. *No baby, no.*

"Na, na, na, na, na, na, na!" Babs keep waving.

"Goddamn it, baby, stop it!" I shout but Babs keep taunting. Keep waving. *They gonna get us, them fuckass punks.* "Stop it," I tell Babs. "The fuckin' collection's all we got. It's all we got. All we got left, yo."

"A miskit, a masket. A dollar in my faskit." Babs mad now, she be pounding the ground.

Shit. Them motherfuckers are shouting again. We scrambling. Scuttling our asses over to the rubble and them fuckers start shooting them boom sticks. AKs popping, *pop, pop, pop, pop, pop, pop.* Raining fucking lead all round.

Bratttttttttttttttt- ta-ta-ta-ta.

"A wiskit ..."

Oh shit, oh shit, oh shit. Babs moaning now. She been hit. *Oh ga-a-a-a-a.* She been fucking hit and the blood coming. *Fuck. Fuck. Fuck.* Babs rocking now. Hugging the collection like baby Jesus and shit. *Goddamnit, she gonna make me cry.*

"Na, na, na, na, na, na," Babs be whispering. "Got us da money."

"I know, Babs. I know it ain't worth shit, but it's ours, baby," I be telling Babs, wrapping them blankets round her belly, pushing the red river back inside my baby. "We got all the fuckin' coins of the realm," I tell her. "We got the treasure. We like fuckin' royalty, baby. We like goddamn queens, yo."

Shit. Now she got me crying good.

"We da queens of all the dollars." Old Babs singing again and them ARs keep *pop, pop, popping* off over yonder.

I sing too, holding my Babs and rocking like she do. "In the land of hoop and holler."

"And da money gonna buy us love ..."

Oh, Babs wiping my eyes now. I be crying and she rocking and wiping my fucking eyes. *That's my girl.*

"Lemme give you some love, darlin'," I tell her. "You done spot that dollar way over yonder, baby girl. Baby Babs girl."

"Comin' at ya, y'all." Babs singing all low-like and I stuff more blankets round her belly. "Hey, hey, Go get a dollar, dollar, a dollar gonna fall from trees."

"You sing it, girl," I tell Babs. "We gonna put all the treasure back, baby. Back in the big red box."

"Goodnight, baby dollar," Babs say and my sweet girl be putting the baby dollar to bed in the box.

"Yeah, baby, you my sweet baby dollar, sweet Baby Babs," I say to Babs and I be crying, holding her and rocking my sweet Baby Babs.

"Lemme give you all we got right here, lemme give da treasure to you." Babs singing but it getting low now, whisper-like.

"We ain't got much of nothing, babe," I sing with Babs, "but it all done come from you."

"Mama don't cry for dollars, girl, 'cause a dollar can't buy me you." Babs keep whisper-singing and she holding me now, hugging me, and we both crying now. We both crying now. *Goddamnit.*

"Yeah, baby," I say to Babs. "Amygda-fucking-la-la-la, baby. You my amygda-fucking-la, girl."

And Babs, she all quiet now. She still. But she still be smiling. Still holding all the coins of the realm.

All Knowledge

One dollar.

Theo had tried to think about moving, about rejoining his brother in the city or his sisters in the suburbs like they swore he must, but each time he'd tried, each time he'd laid his book down and walked to the dresser by the window to pack, he'd seen it.

The sign: *All the Great Books You Can Carry—$1.00*

Two years into his grand adventure, his great escape from the hustle, the relentless roar of ambition that ricocheted around him, that menacing world his parents and teachers and siblings insisted was the best and only path in life, that sign still made him swoon.

All the Great Books You Can Carry—$1.00

Oh, what a feast it's been, a banquet, a fete. And isn't still? Nevermind what they said, what his sisters and brothers proclaimed as the truth, about money and meaning and the real world and all. *Why can't it go on,* he thought and rethought, *this banquet of stories, for the rest of my life?*

Theo looked again at the certified letter that had arrived that morning from his sister's lawyer. "You are hereby mandated to appear ..." it said and summoned him for a "Compulsory Psychological Evaluation" at such and such a date and time and place.

And there, taped to the envelope was a note from his landlady: *What does this mean, Theo?* she'd written in her wobbly hand. *Are you in some kind of trouble?*

He felt faint and slumped down in front of the sagging mahogany drawers, filled with the corduroy pants and t-shirts and sweaters he'd worn all these years. He closed his eyes and lay flat on the floor the way he had as a boy when the world was too much with him then as it was now. He ran his long fingers over the ribs of the braided rug that stretched from the bed to the dresser. His stomach churned as it used to do in the libraries of his childhood, and he curled his bony knees up under his chin.

He'd done it again, he realized, forgotten to eat. "Now Theo," his mother used to scold him. "Put that book down, child, and eat. A growing boy needs real food, not just food for thought."

"Not now, Mom," he'd tell her, the high seas pounding his ears, Quequeq's coffin bobbing before him. "I am Ishmael, just let me be!"

His stomach growled again, and Theo opened his eyes. In his sparsely furnished room, stacked all around the walls, jammed under the dresser, and behind the box of letters from his family were his treasures, his prizes, keepers of all knowledge, his true and only friends. Borges and Rumi, Pushkin, Camus, Dunbar and Orwell, Maugham, Angelou. Gently, he slid a stack out onto the expanse of the floor. Nestled behind them, in neat, perfect rows were their brethren—Goethe, Gibran, Baldwin and Bontemps, Bradbury, Hughes, Cervantes and Ellison, Achebe and Dante, Toomer and Homer and Woolf.

"I can't do it," he whispered, his heart again burdened. So much sorrow they'd been through, he and his heroes. So much strife and betrayal. War and rebellion. Redemption and love. "I can't leave you," he said, stroking their spines.

He sat and looked through the letters, pleading with him over the years to stop his bookish nonsense and come back into their world.

"Dear Theo," the letters always began. "Enough is enough, bro," his brother Andre had written.

"You're squandering your education," wrote his sister Renee.

"Think of your mother," his father had begged him.

"Come home, my sweet Theo," his mother had implored. "We'll find you a righteous real job."

"Don't make us do it," his sister Wanda had said, her bossy, big-sister voice coming through in her words. "We *will* meet with that lawyer. We'll do it. You have got to come home."

Theo thought of Ivan Denisovich in his Siberian gulag, clutching his crust of bread, taking joy in the smallest of pleasures: the butt of a cigarette, a small bowl of kasha, a moment of sleep, and Theo knew his family was wrong. *They're all wrong.*

Here, Theo thought, *in this room, it is warm, is it not,* and he gave a sweet, silent thanks to the old man and old woman who swapped him this room and his meals for some labor, such as it was, mowing grass, chopping wood, hanging wash.

Simple work, simple life.

He thought of the diner where he swept up off and again, for a dollar or four or a hot cup of joe at the counter to crack open a new book.

What more do I need?

He breathed in and thought of the blind poet Borges and his labyrinths, and of Tillie Olsen standing there ironing. Of Toomer's women living alone in the thin strip of land between the tracks where the pines sing to Jesus. Of the Invisible Man with his hundreds of light bulbs in his underground room, and Theo's heart ached the ache of a thousand stories held close while the wind hurled itself against the night and the sparrows sought refuge in the splintered wood outside his window.

He closed his eyes and Whitman, leaning and loafing at his ease, summoned him to lie down among the blades of summer grass.

"The beautiful uncut hair of graves," Theo muttered and kneeled on his knees. He slid the yellowing stacks of paperbacks back under the dresser, lining them up in quaint, even rows like potted pansies. "Tenderly will I use you curling grass," he whispered and fumbled in his pocket.

There, crumpled between a book of spent matches and an Indian penny he'd found on the road, was an old dollar bill, change from the five-spot he'd made Monday sweeping the diner's front porch.

"One dollar more." He rose to his feet and checked the clock on the wall. One hour before the bookstore closed.

One hour. One dollar.

For all the knowledge in the world.

Theo ripped up the summons, put on his jacket, and headed for the door.

Acknowledgments

In the many years I spent writing these one-dollar stories, I am indebted to so many people. Deepest thanks to my writing group colleagues with whom I shared or created these works—Joy Jones, Phil Kurata, Tom Adams, Cheryl Miner, Shabnam Arora Afsah, Sarah Pleydell, Debra Bowling, Janelle Williams, Louise Baxter, Anne Pelliciotto, and Writers on the Green Line. To David A. Taylor for his early full manuscript read and Naomi Ayala for constant support. To all who took the time to give me supportive remarks, and to the editors of all the journals and anthologies that published these stories before. To the cast and crew of "Legal Tender: Flash Theatre for a Flash Fiction World" for enlivening early stories on stage. To the DC Commission on the Arts & Humanities for the fellowships that fortified my writing life. To CentroNía for being an anchor in my life. To Jessica Bell, Amie McCracken, Melanie Faith, and everyone at Vine Leaves Press for their extraordinary expertise. To my childhood best friend, the late Gladys Hunter Lauzon Bohannon, for an early life of rule-breaking, belly laughs, and high adventure in our little Texas town. And especially to my beloved husband and creative partner Robert Michael Oliver for his literary X-ray vision, sage counsel, and our life-long creative partnership. And to Maya and Nico and Dylan and Megan and our and their extended families for their resonant friendships and support. Thank you, thank you all.

Grateful acknowledgement is made to the following publications in the USA, UK, Canada, Australia, New Zealand, Sweden, India, South Korea, The Philippines, Yemen, and Malawi in which some of these stories appeared, sometimes in slightly different forms: "Sweat," "Grocery List," and "The Gutter," *Vine Leaves Journal Anthology: A Collection of Vignettes from Across the Globe* (Australia); "Universally Adored," *Academy Press/The Atherton Review* (USA) and with "Evening in Paris" in *The Library of Colors* of The Aerogramme Center (USA); "Bald Tires," *FireWords Quarterly* (UK) and also published as a reprint at *The Song Is …* (USA); "Little Jimmy," *BareBack Magazine* (USA); "Van Camp's Pork & Beans," *Gargoyle 64: An Anthology,* Paycock Press (USA); The Grass Jesus Walked On," *Literally Stories* (UK) and *Muddy Backroads: Stories from Off the Beaten Path,* Madville Publishing (USA); "Magic Fingers," *'Merica Magazine* (USA); "Primin' the Pump" and "Cargo Pants." *Pure Slush* (Australia); "The Bell," *The Dead Mule School of Southern Literature* (USA); Ricky Steiner Was Supposed To Die in Prison," *Gargoyle 75: An Anthology,*

Paycock Press (USA), "MOUSE SOCKS," *Samjoko Magazine* (South Korea); "FLOUNDER" and "THE TUESDAY THEORY" (now titled), *The Remembered Arts* (USA); "FLOUNDER," (published as a reprint) *ppigpen.blogspot* (USA); "BOOGIE BOARD," *Inklette* (USA); "AIRPORT CADDY," *Eos: The Creative Context* (USA); "ICE COLD WATER," *The Elixir Magazine* (Yemen); "STARRY LASHES," *Attic Door Press* (USA); "THE TUESDAY THEORY" (published as a reprint), *The Nthanda Review* (Malawi); "GAS STATION," *takahē magazine* (New Zealand); "THE FORGIVENESS MAN," *This Is What America Looks Like,* anthology from Washington Writers' Publishing House (USA); "EXACT CHANGE ONLY," *Degenerate Literature* (USA); "DOLORES," *Spadina Literary Review* (Canada), which nominated it for a 2018 Pushcart Prize; "BOILING THE BUGGERS," *Anvil Tongue Books* (USA); "VOTIVE CANDLE," *The Bangalore Review* (India); "BLOODY RABBIT," *Two Thirds North 2023* (Sweden); "MASHED POTATOES," *Smoky Quartz* (USA); "FESTUS," *The McKinley Review* (The Philippines); "AMYGDALA-LA-LA," *How Well You Walk through Madness: An Anthology of Beat,* Weasel Press (USA); and "ALL KNOWLEDGE," *The Olive Press* (USA).

Grateful acknowledgement is also made to Sanctuary Theatre, Inc., and the Capital Fringe Theatre Festival. In 2013 Sanctuary Theatre's Performing Knowledge Project adapted nine of the short fictions included in this collection into "Prose-in-Performance" scripts, in which the focal characters, subjective and interior narrative voices, voices of backstory or present action characters, and objective narrative and authorial voices were delineated in script form and animated on stage by an ensemble of five actors. The text of the scripts exactly mirrored the prose and even included dialogue tags. Sanctuary Theatre Artistic Director Robert Michael Oliver co-authored these adaptations for the stage with Elizabeth Bruce. The production, entitled "Legal Tender: Flash Theatre for a Flash Fiction World," was produced at the 2013 Capital Fringe Festival in Washington, DC, and included "LITTLE JIMMY," "THE GUTTER." "VAN CAMP'S PORK & BEANS," "MAGIC FINGERS," "AIRPORT CADDY," "CARGO PANTS," "GAS STATION," "EXACT CHANGE ONLY," and "PRIMIN' THE PUMP." The cast included Sharyce L. McElvane, Maya C. Oliver, Forest Rilling, Rachel Viele, and Andrew White, with sound design and stage management by Elliot Lanes.

Vine Leaves Press

Enjoyed this book?
Go to *vineleavespress.com* to find more.
Subscribe to our newsletter: